image COMICS PRESENTS

INVINCIBLE

FAMILY MATTERS

CREATED BY
ROBERT KIRKMAN
& CORY WALKER

image

Writer, Letterer
Robert Kirkman

Penciler, Inker
Cory Walker

Colorist
Bill Crabtree

IMAGE COMICS, INC.
www.imagecomics.com

ERIK LARSEN
Publisher
TODD McFARLANE
President
MARC SILVESTRI
CEO
JIM VALENTINO
Vice-President
ERIC STEPHENSON
Executive Director
JIM DEMONAKOS
PR & Marketing Coordinator
MIA MacHATTON
Accounts Manager
TRACI HUI
Administrative Assistant
JOE KEATINGE
Traffic Manager
ALLEN HUI
Production Manager
JONATHAN CHAN
Production Artist
DREW GILL
Production Artist
CHRIS GIARRUSSO
Production Artist

THE EVIL THAT IS ROBERT KIRKMAN

Run. Run, and whatever you do, don't look back.
-- Erik Larsen

Listen to me. For the love of God, listen to me. Don't try to understand it.
Just go. And go quickly.
-- Eric Stephenson

It's too late – too late for us. Leave us -- just save yourself.
-- Jim Valentino

If only I'd listened.

Understand something. I don't know Robert Kirkman. I've never met Robert Kirkman, at least not that I'm aware of. He could be six foot two, with a full head of wavy blond hair, a cleft in his chin and the build of a champion surfer. But that's not how I think of him. I think of him as about four foot eight and hydrocephalic, with a head like a pumpkin. Lank thin hair, beady little eyes, and a shriveled body that you'd barely think could hold that enormous head up. And his voice. One of those voices like nails on a blackboard, that suddenly shrills out behind you when you were thinking of something else, and you're halfway to the ceiling, nerves on fire, before you even realize what you've heard.

If only I'd listened.

*

But no, here I am.

Like the vast majority of smart-thinking Americans, I passed up Invincible #1 at least twice. Heard about the new Image "superhero line," saw the books in the catalog, and breezed right by Invincible. Just another superhero book, I thought. I've got a complete run of *Nova*. Of *Firestorm*. Of *Speedball*, for Pete's sake. This isn't anything I need. Firebreather, that's what I went for. *Firebreather* and *Dominion*.

Smart man.

And then the books came out, and there I was in the comics shop, and there was Invincible, and I passed it up again. Didn't even pick it up and flip through it. Just another superhero cover, nothing special, don't bother.

Ah, for the days of freedom. Were they really only months ago?

*

So here I am, writing introductions, suggesting cover copy, even coming up with cover concepts (like the one for the cover to the volume you currently hold in your hot little imperiled hands). And all for free. All for that pumpkin-headed freak with the chalkboard voice, who cackles – I just know it, I know he cackles – as I slave away for his benefit.

I'm an Eisner Award-winning writer, for the love of heaven. A Harvey Award-winner! Multiple times over! I have interview requests to disdain, characters to abuse, fan hopes to dash. I have artists to torment, editors who still cling to faint hopes of getting me to do something on time! I'm a busy man!

And yet here I am, working for Kirkman when I could be getting *Astro City* out monthly. When *Avengers/JLA* could already be out. When I could be reading classic Little Lulu issues to my daughters. But no.

Kirkman. Goddamn Kirkman.

*

I ignored the warning signs. I saw people talking about Invincible on Erik Larsen's message board, but I missed that hysterical, compulsive undertone. I saw someone point out that the entire first issue was available to be read for free at the Image website. I figured what the hell, it's free, right?

Nothing's free. I should have listened to Larsen.

I went over to the Image site and I read it. Went back to the Larsen site to comment. Mostly just to rag on that first cover, which I thought was a big mistake, if you must know. And now look at me.

*

The thing is – and this is the dark secret they don't want you to know until it's too late – Kirkman's good. Really good.

Invincible is fun, fresh, energetic. It's not one of those superhero books that doesn't want to admit to liking superheroes, so it tries to put a different spin on it and winds up being an uncomfortable mélange of nothing. No, Invincible embraces its genre. It's a superhero book that loves being a superhero book, one that isn't out to deconstruct or expose or undermine or scathingly satirize. It just wants to be a good superhero book. And yet, it still manages to put a different spin on things, and winds up being distinctive and clever and alive, all the while standing foursquare at the heart of a longstanding, well-worked genre that many would say has nothing more to offer.

If only.

I think my favorite character is Mark's mom. Her casual acceptance of her family life, her tension when her "boys" are out of touch even by the reach of CNN, her matter-of-factness about the fantastic, that's the glue that makes this book work. I want to see an annual, *Invincible's Mom, Debbie Grayson*. It's that aspect – not contrast, but melding – of Mark's two worlds that makes Invincible so compelling.

It'd be okay if that was all there was to it. A new good comic? Fine, bring it on.

But Kirkman is relentless. Invincible led me to *Tech Jacket*. To the *Superpatriot* series he and Cory Walker did. To *Battle Pope*. And now there's *Brit* coming up. And *Capes*. And *Masters of the Universe*.

Masters of the Universe, for cryin' out loud!

And then there are the artists. Cory Walker is the one we're concerned about here, and his clean, clear storytelling, his deadpan characterization, his sleek designs, his distinctive, stylized rendering ... it all brings the book to life in a way that'll make you feel you know these people. That you could sit down and have a conversation with them, at least while you weren't surreptitiously checking out Atom Eve's butt.

But there's E.J. Su on *Tech Jacket*. Tony Moore on *Battle Pope* and *Brit*. And they're all good. All distinctive, clear, solid, compelling. Where does he find these guys?

It's not natural, I tell you.

*

So here you are. You may still have a choice. Maybe you're someone who's already been reading *Invincible*, and those proliferating other books. If so, never mind. You're as gone as I am, one of the chittering wrecks on the message board, unable resist trying to pass on your addiction, share it with the unwary. But maybe you just heard the buzz, or picked this up in the store because of that cool cover concept, or something. If so, then there's still time.

You're standing on the precipice, like I was. You can put this back on the shelf, back away slowly, and get on with your life. Or if you've already purchased the book, but you're just reading the intro before you get into the stories, well ... you probably have a furnace, don't you?

Because otherwise, you'll take that step. You'll take it, and there'll be no turning back. You'll get swept up into Kirkman's world, one more helpless victim unable to break free, hopelessly drawn to each new release, to each new character, caught on tenterhooks between episodes, as you wait to see what'll happen next. Just one more Funk-O-Drone. You'll be recommending the book to friends, spreading the word online. You might even end up working for that hellish fiend for free.

He'll have you, then. And Kirkman doesn't let go.

*

So listen to me. Listen carefully. Like I should have listened, when I was where you are now. But no, I was cocky. Confident. Foolish. *Doomed*.

It's too late for me. But you -- you can still get away. Can warn others.

Put the book down. Back away. For God's sake, don't turn that page.

And if you do, then remember this, in those still small hours:

I warned you.

-- Kurt Busiek
May 2003

KURT BUSIEK has enough awards plaques to tile his bathroom, and enough damn statuettes to play chess on the result. He writes, in theory, for Marvel, DC, Wildstorm, Dark Horse and more. In fact, he should be doing paying work right now.

Think of the children, won't you? The children.

CHAPTER ONE

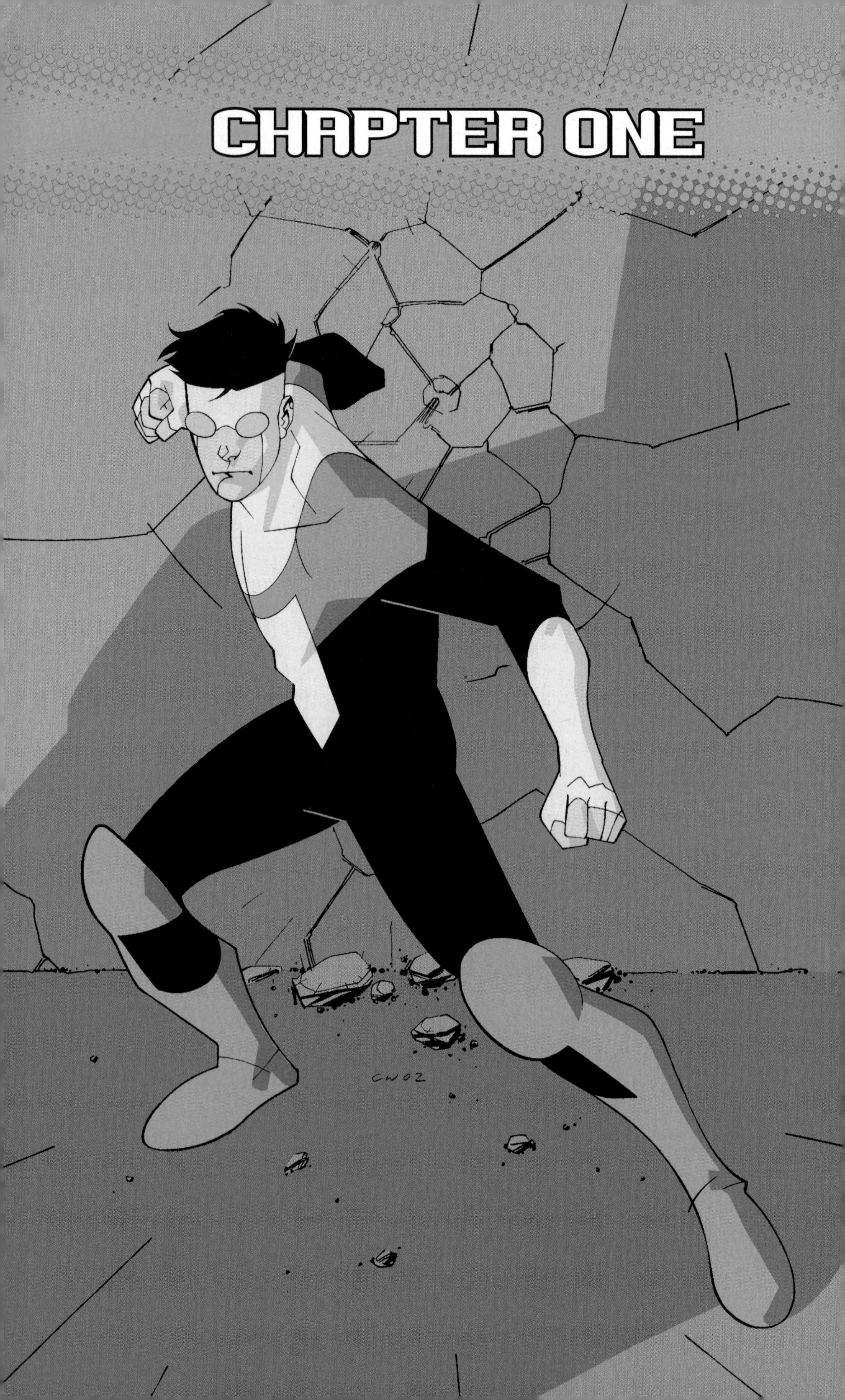

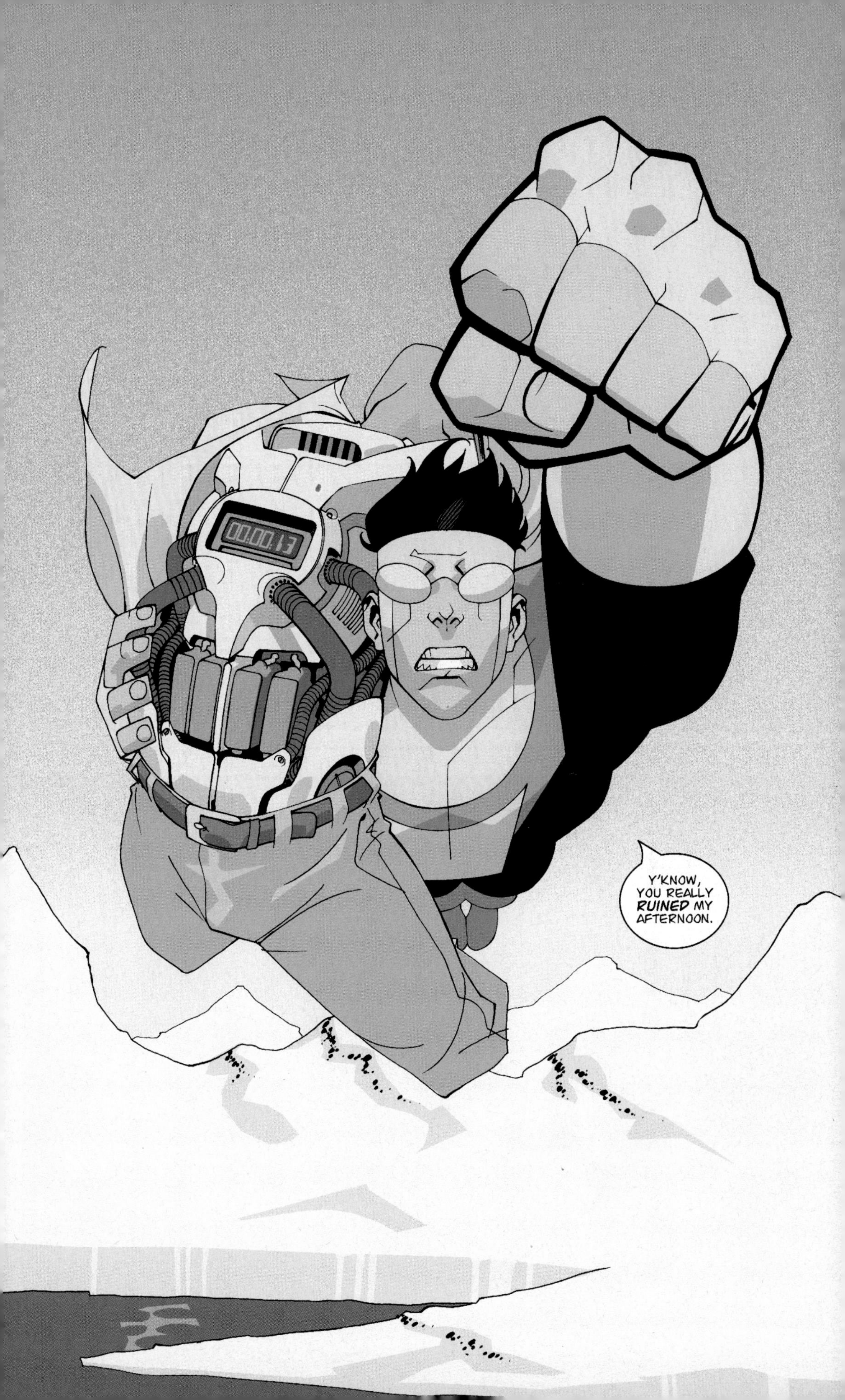
Y'KNOW, YOU REALLY RUINED MY AFTERNOON.

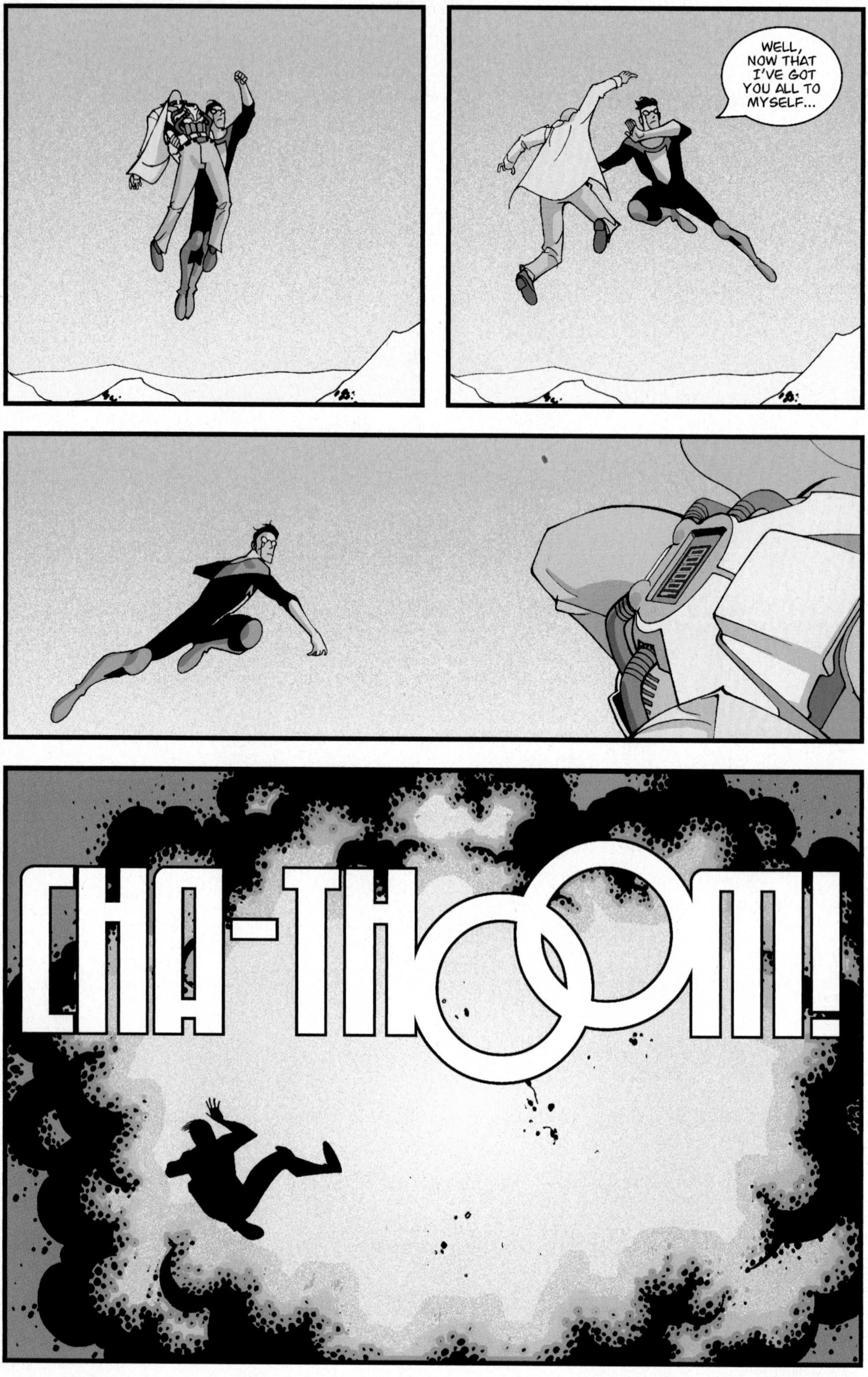
WELL, NOW THAT I'VE GOT YOU ALL TO MYSELF...
CHA-THOOM!

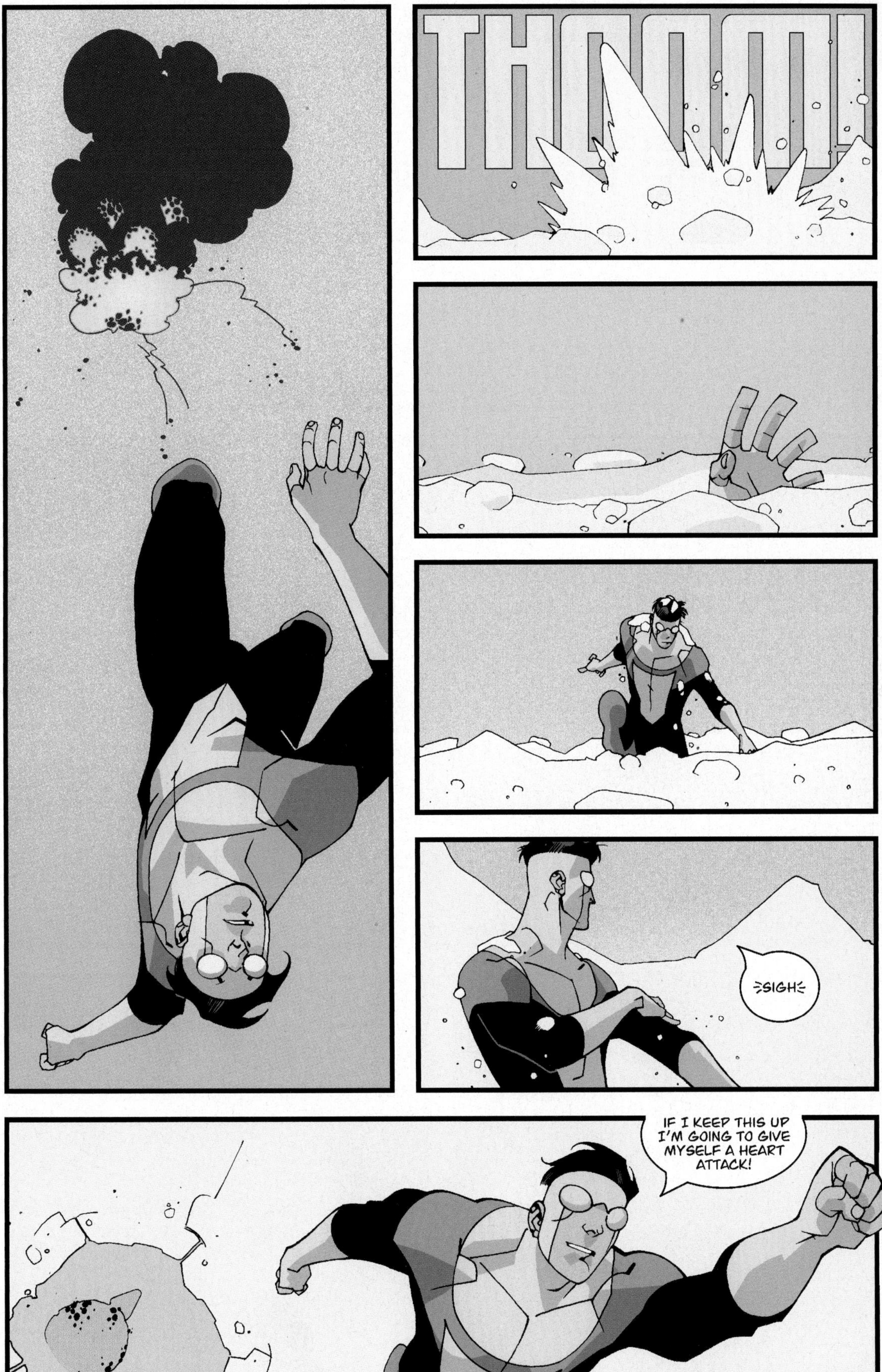
THOOM!
=SIGH=
IF I KEEP THIS UP I'M GOING TO GIVE MYSELF A HEART ATTACK!

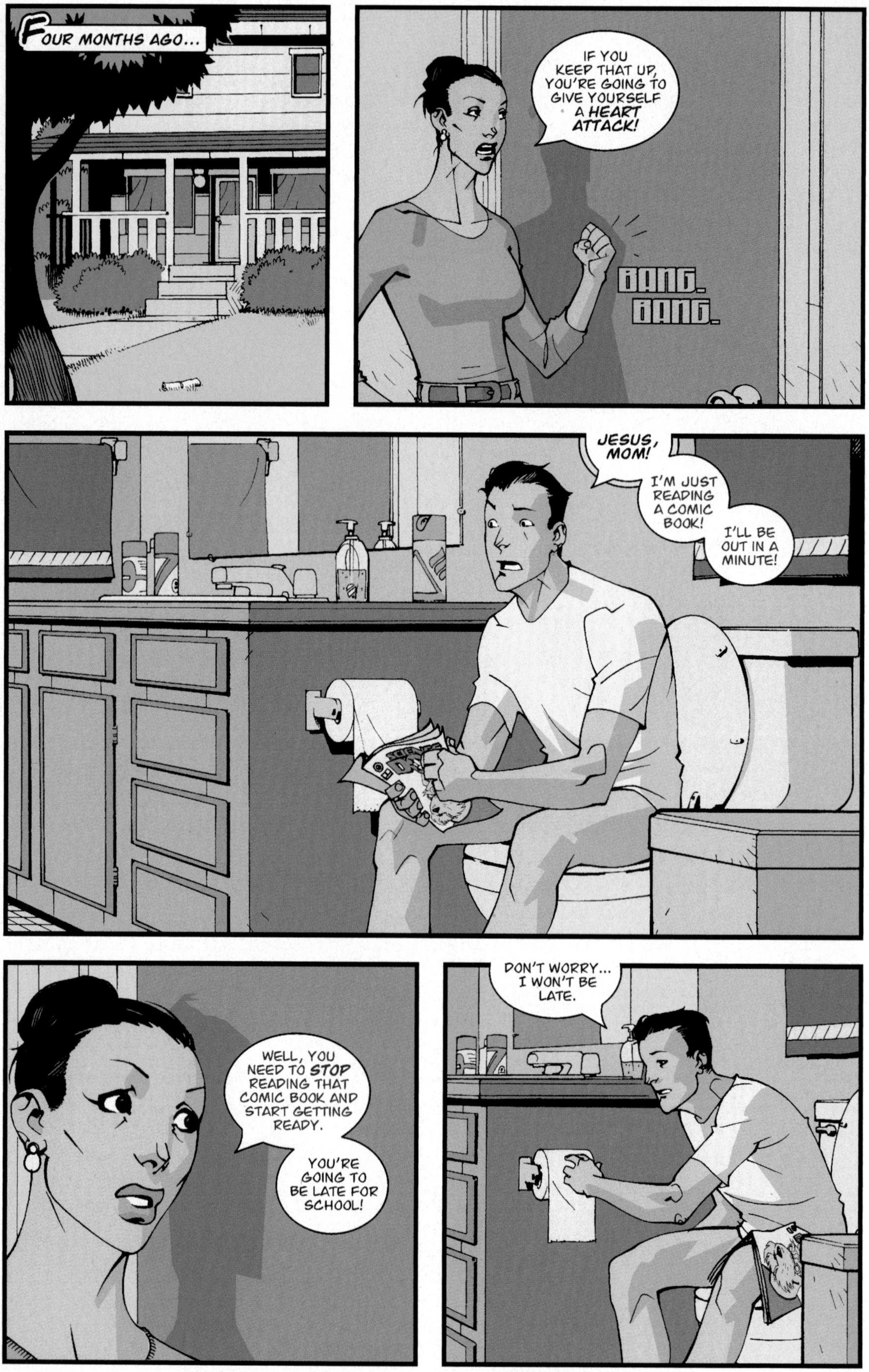
FOUR MONTHS AGO...
IF YOU KEEP THAT UP, YOU'RE GOING TO GIVE YOURSELF A HEART ATTACK!
BANG. BANG.
JESUS, MOM!
I'M JUST READING A COMIC BOOK!
I'LL BE OUT IN A MINUTE!
WELL, YOU NEED TO STOP READING THAT COMIC BOOK AND START GETTING READY.
YOU'RE GOING TO BE LATE FOR SCHOOL!
DON'T WORRY... I WON'T BE LATE.

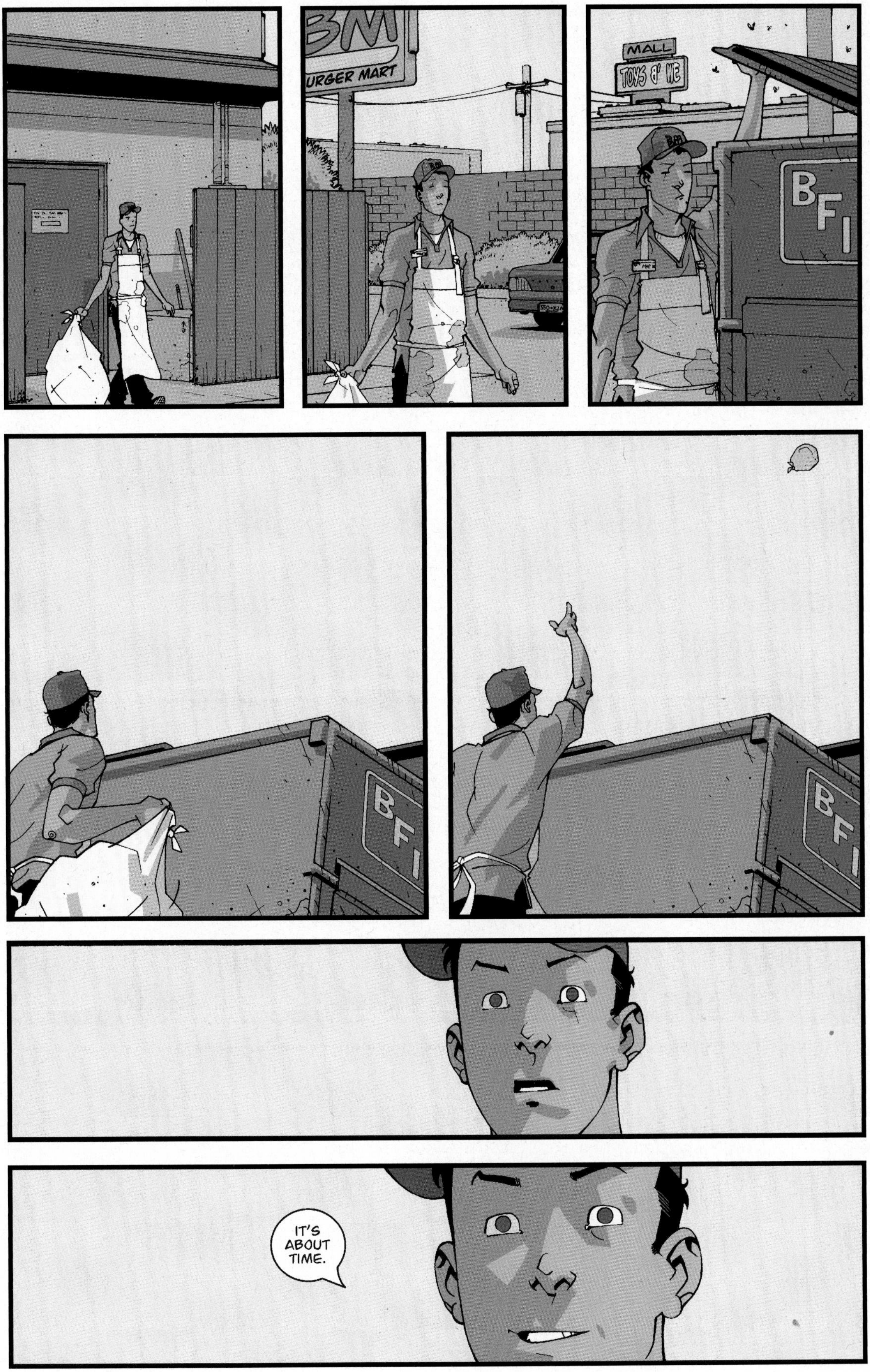
BM
BURGER MART
MALL
TOYS & WE
BFI
BFI
BFI
IT'S ABOUT TIME.

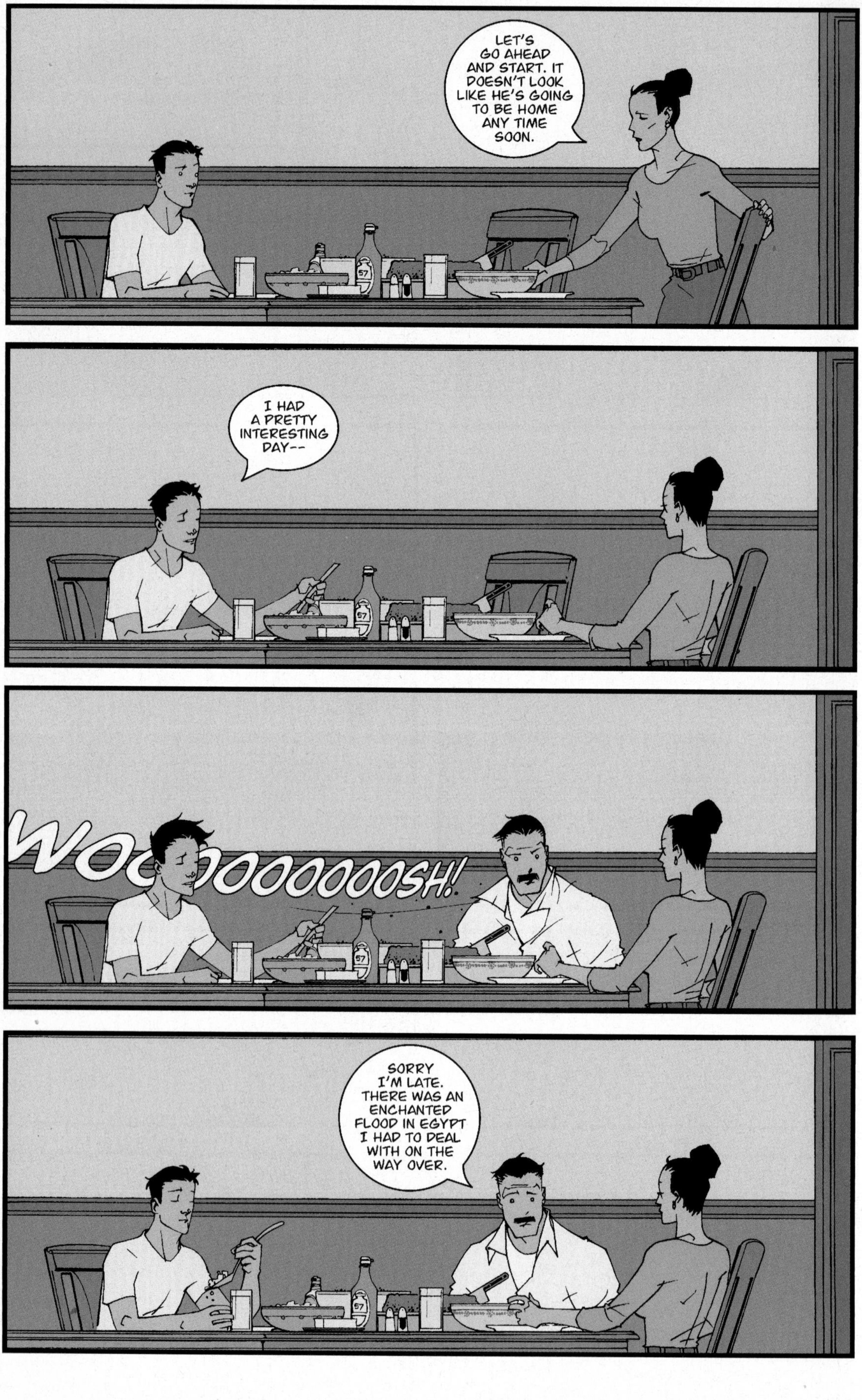
LET'S GO AHEAD AND START. IT DOESN'T LOOK LIKE HE'S GOING TO BE HOME ANY TIME SOON.
I HAD A PRETTY INTERESTING DAY--
WOOOOOOOOOOSH!
SORRY I'M LATE. THERE WAS AN ENCHANTED FLOOD IN EGYPT I HAD TO DEAL WITH ON THE WAY OVER.

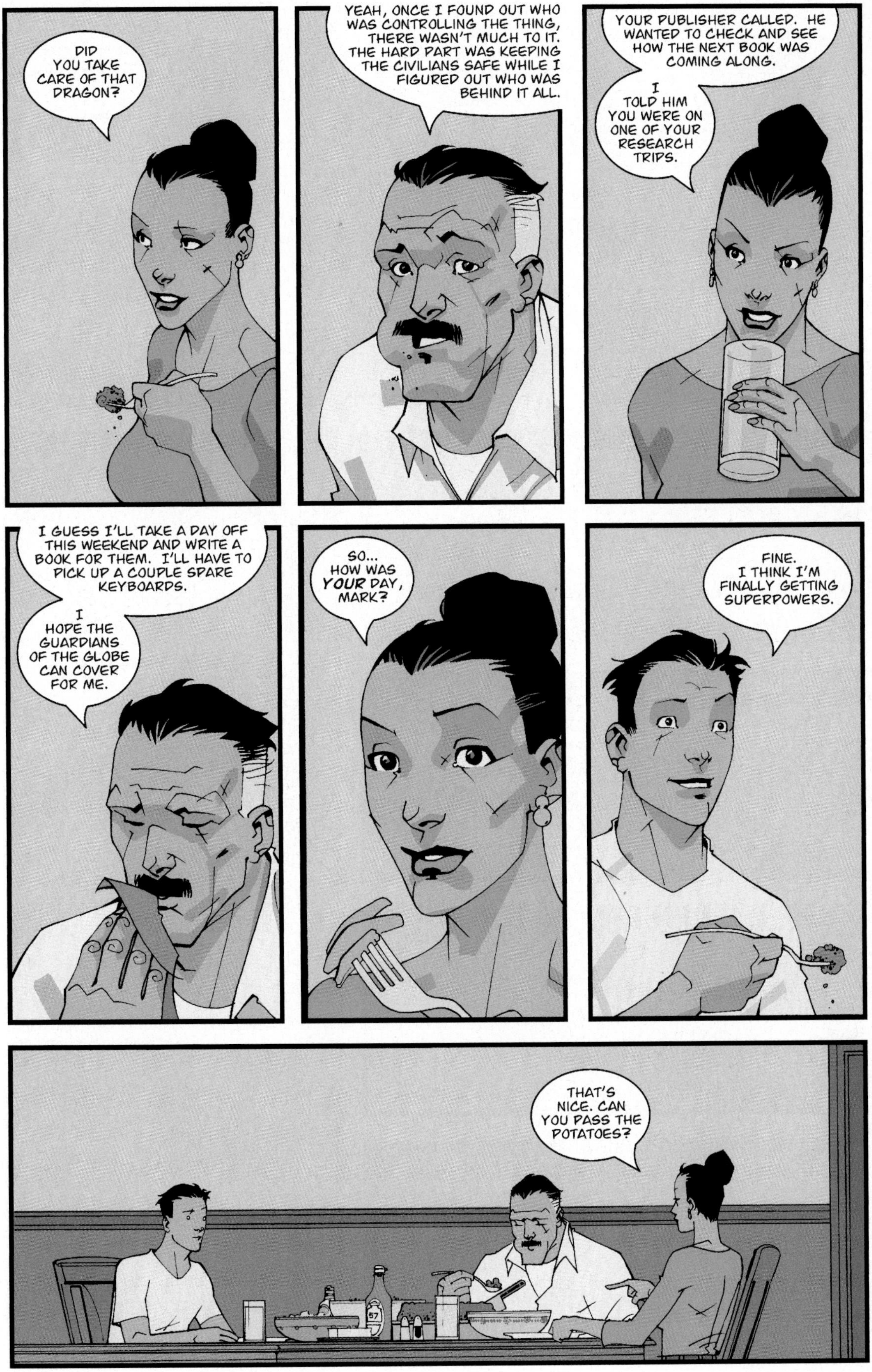
DID YOU TAKE CARE OF THAT DRAGON?
YEAH, ONCE I FOUND OUT WHO WAS CONTROLLING THE THING, THERE WASN'T MUCH TO IT. THE HARD PART WAS KEEPING THE CIVILIANS SAFE WHILE I FIGURED OUT WHO WAS BEHIND IT ALL.
YOUR PUBLISHER CALLED. HE WANTED TO CHECK AND SEE HOW THE NEXT BOOK WAS COMING ALONG.
I TOLD HIM YOU WERE ON ONE OF YOUR RESEARCH TRIPS.
I GUESS I'LL TAKE A DAY OFF THIS WEEKEND AND WRITE A BOOK FOR THEM. I'LL HAVE TO PICK UP A COUPLE SPARE KEYBOARDS.
I HOPE THE GUARDIANS OF THE GLOBE CAN COVER FOR ME.
SO... HOW WAS YOUR DAY, MARK?
FINE. I THINK I'M FINALLY GETTING SUPERPOWERS.
THAT'S NICE. CAN YOU PASS THE POTATOES?

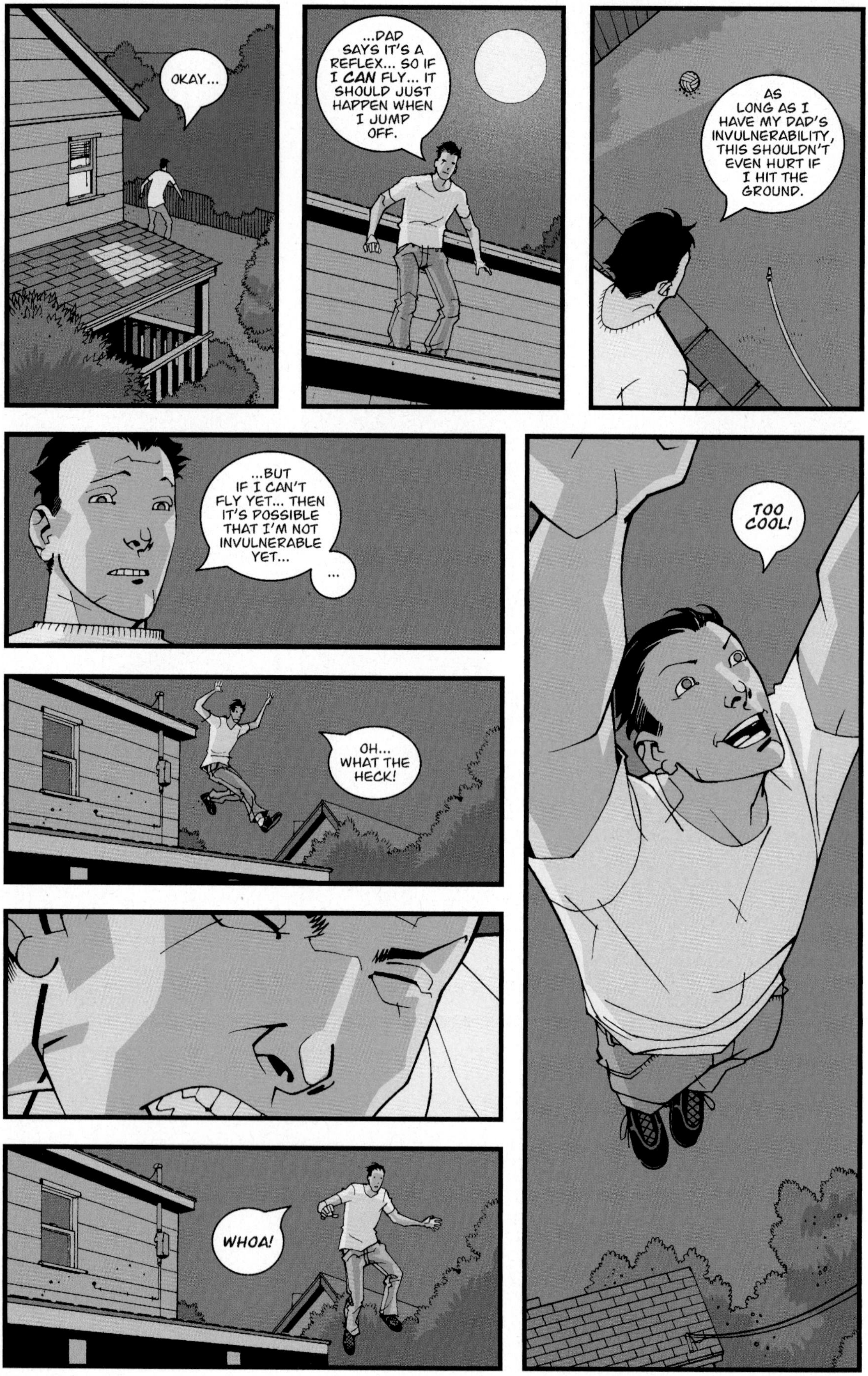
OKAY...
...DAD SAYS IT'S A REFLEX... SO IF I CAN FLY... IT SHOULD JUST HAPPEN WHEN I JUMP OFF.
AS LONG AS I HAVE MY DAD'S INVULNERABILITY, THIS SHOULDN'T EVEN HURT IF I HIT THE GROUND.
...BUT IF I CAN'T FLY YET... THEN IT'S POSSIBLE THAT I'M NOT INVULNERABLE YET...
...
OH... WHAT THE HECK!
WHOA!
TOO COOL!

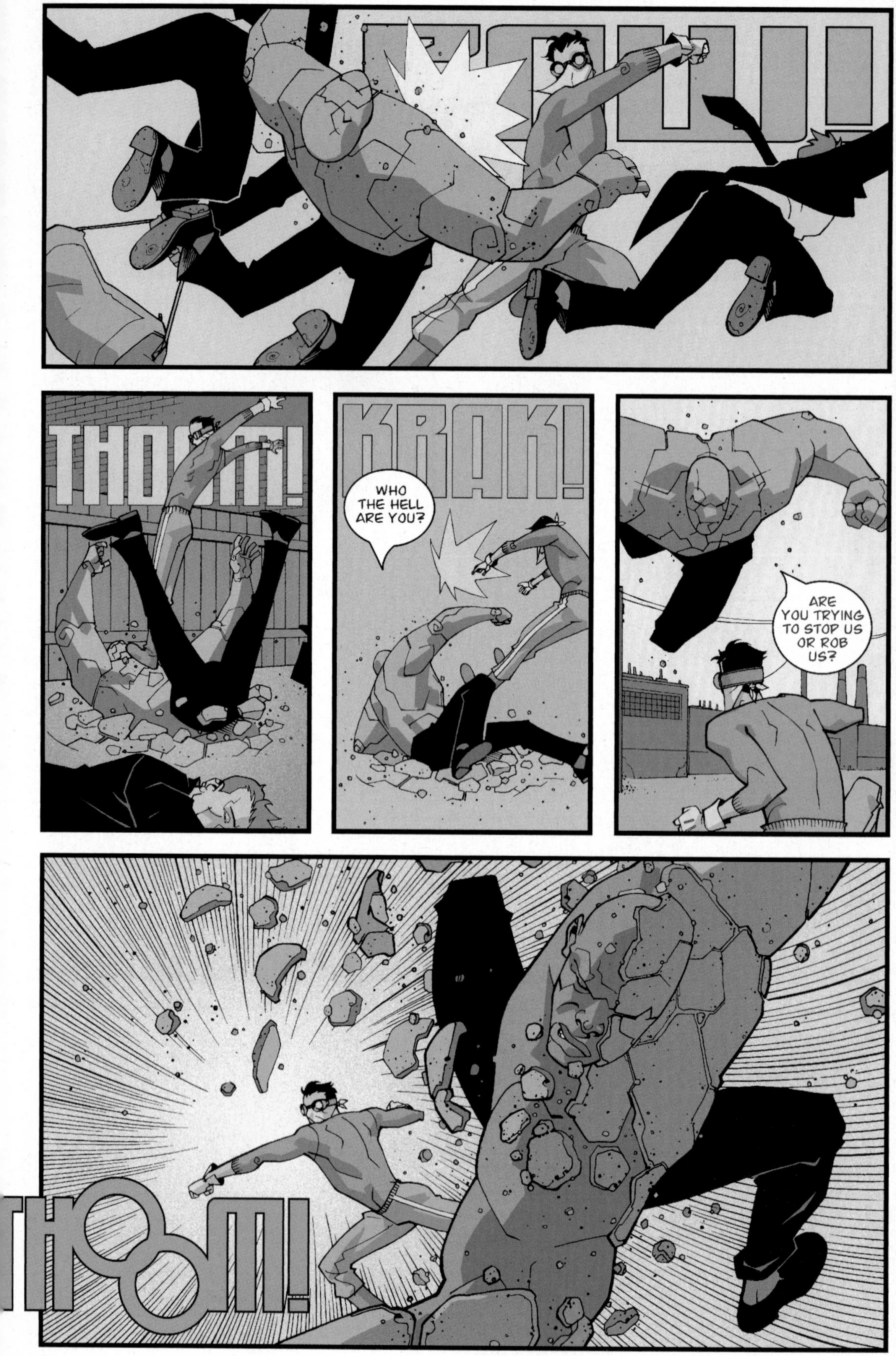
THOOM!
KRAK!
WHO THE HELL ARE YOU?
ARE YOU TRYING TO STOP US OR ROB US?
THOOM!

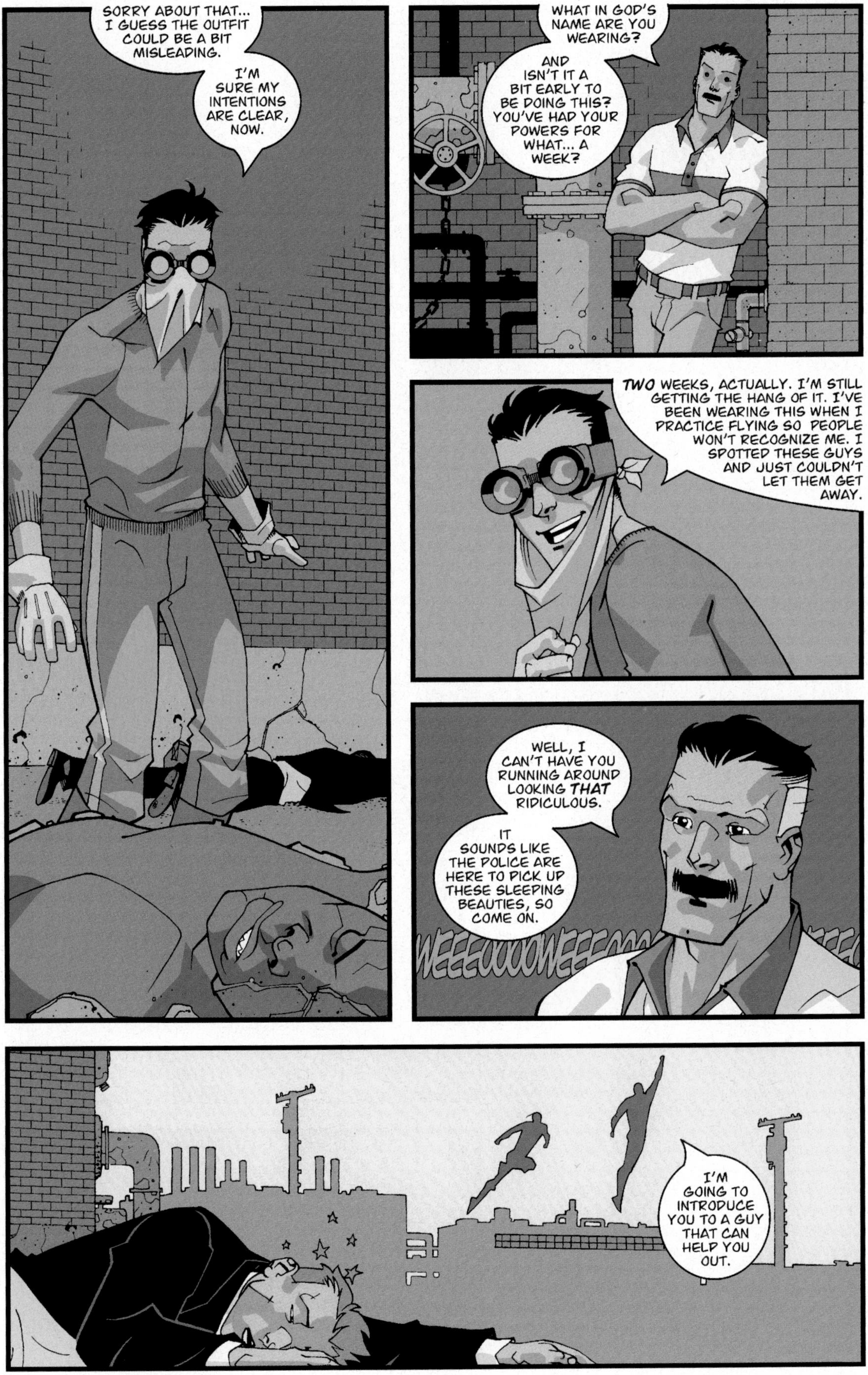
SORRY ABOUT THAT... I GUESS THE OUTFIT COULD BE A BIT MISLEADING.
I'M SURE MY INTENTIONS ARE CLEAR, NOW.
WHAT IN GOD'S NAME ARE YOU WEARING?
AND ISN'T IT A BIT EARLY TO BE DOING THIS? YOU'VE HAD YOUR POWERS FOR WHAT... A WEEK?
TWO WEEKS, ACTUALLY. I'M STILL GETTING THE HANG OF IT. I'VE BEEN WEARING THIS WHEN I PRACTICE FLYING SO PEOPLE WON'T RECOGNIZE ME. I SPOTTED THESE GUYS AND JUST COULDN'T LET THEM GET AWAY.
WELL, I CAN'T HAVE YOU RUNNING AROUND LOOKING *THAT* RIDICULOUS.
IT SOUNDS LIKE THE POLICE ARE HERE TO PICK UP THESE SLEEPING BEAUTIES, SO COME ON.
I'M GOING TO INTRODUCE YOU TO A GUY THAT CAN HELP YOU OUT.

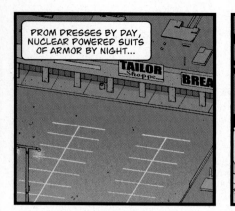

PROM DRESSES BY DAY, NUCLEAR POWERED SUITS OF ARMOR BY NIGHT...

...WITH YOUR STANDARD SPANDEX NUMBER THROWN IN EVERY NOW AND THEN FOR GOOD MEASURE.

I'VE HAD THIS SECRET WORKSHOP HERE FOREVER.

WELL... HOW DOES IT FEEL?

I DON'T KNOW ABOUT THIS ORANGE AND YELLOW. I MEAN, IT SINGS... BUT I DON'T THINK IT'S THE TUNE WE'RE LOOKING FOR.

AND WHAT'S WITH ALL THESE WEIRD DISK THINGS?

THEY'RE SOLAR BATTERIES. I DESIGNED THAT COSTUME BACK WHEN I WAS UNDER THE IMPRESSION THAT YOU AND YOUR DAD'S POWERS WERE SOLAR POWER BASED.

IT'S A COMMON MISTAKE, DON'T WORRY ABOUT IT.

CRAP, GRIDLOCK IS TEARING UP THE EAST SIDE BRIDGE! I'VE GOT TO GO!

USE THE NORTH--!

WHOOOOOOSH!

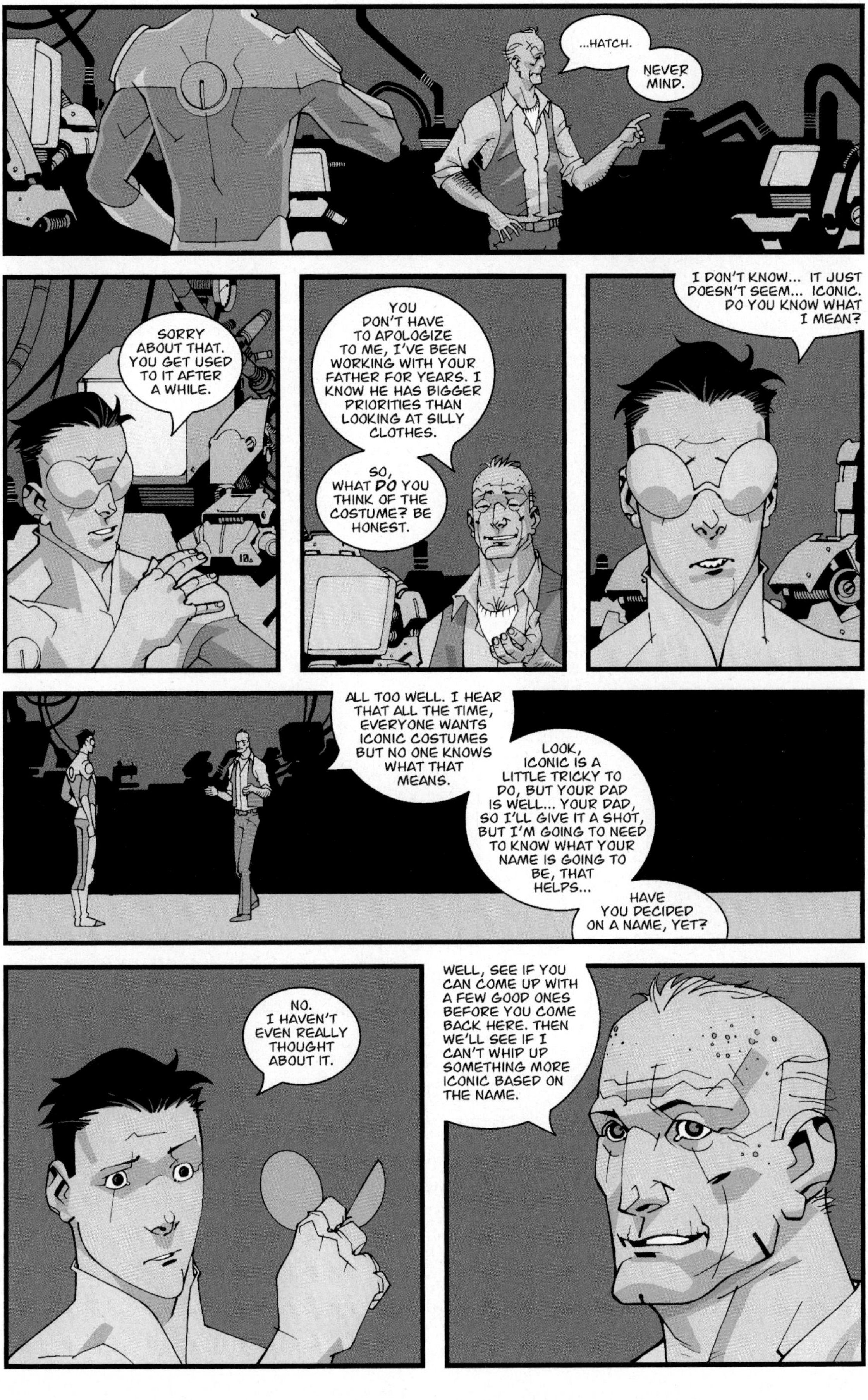
...HATCH.
NEVER MIND.
SORRY ABOUT THAT. YOU GET USED TO IT AFTER A WHILE.
YOU DON'T HAVE TO APOLOGIZE TO ME, I'VE BEEN WORKING WITH YOUR FATHER FOR YEARS. I KNOW HE HAS BIGGER PRIORITIES THAN LOOKING AT SILLY CLOTHES.
SO, WHAT **DO** YOU THINK OF THE COSTUME? BE HONEST.
I DON'T KNOW... IT JUST DOESN'T SEEM... ICONIC. DO YOU KNOW WHAT I MEAN?
ALL TOO WELL. I HEAR THAT ALL THE TIME, EVERYONE WANTS ICONIC COSTUMES BUT NO ONE KNOWS WHAT THAT MEANS.
LOOK, ICONIC IS A LITTLE TRICKY TO DO, BUT YOUR DAD IS WELL... YOUR DAD, SO I'LL GIVE IT A SHOT, BUT I'M GOING TO NEED TO KNOW WHAT YOUR NAME IS GOING TO BE, THAT HELPS...
HAVE YOU DECIDED ON A NAME, YET?
NO. I HAVEN'T EVEN REALLY THOUGHT ABOUT IT.
WELL, SEE IF YOU CAN COME UP WITH A FEW GOOD ONES BEFORE YOU COME BACK HERE. THEN WE'LL SEE IF I CAN'T WHIP UP SOMETHING MORE ICONIC BASED ON THE NAME.

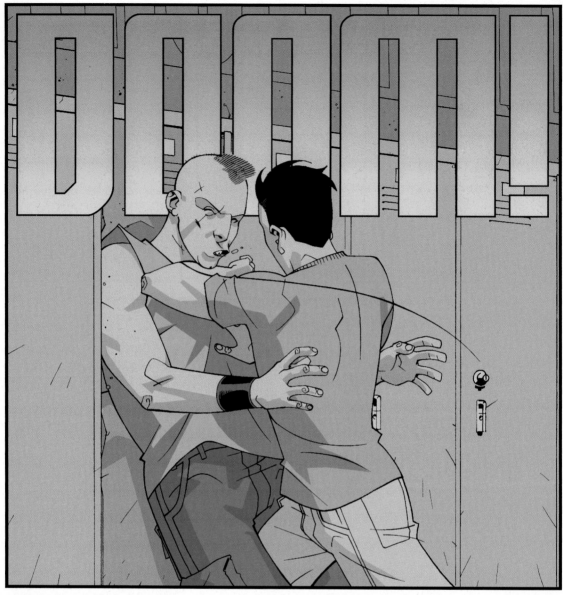

UGH...

DON'T MESS WITH HIM AGAIN, MAN.

WHAT THE HECK IS GOING ON HERE?

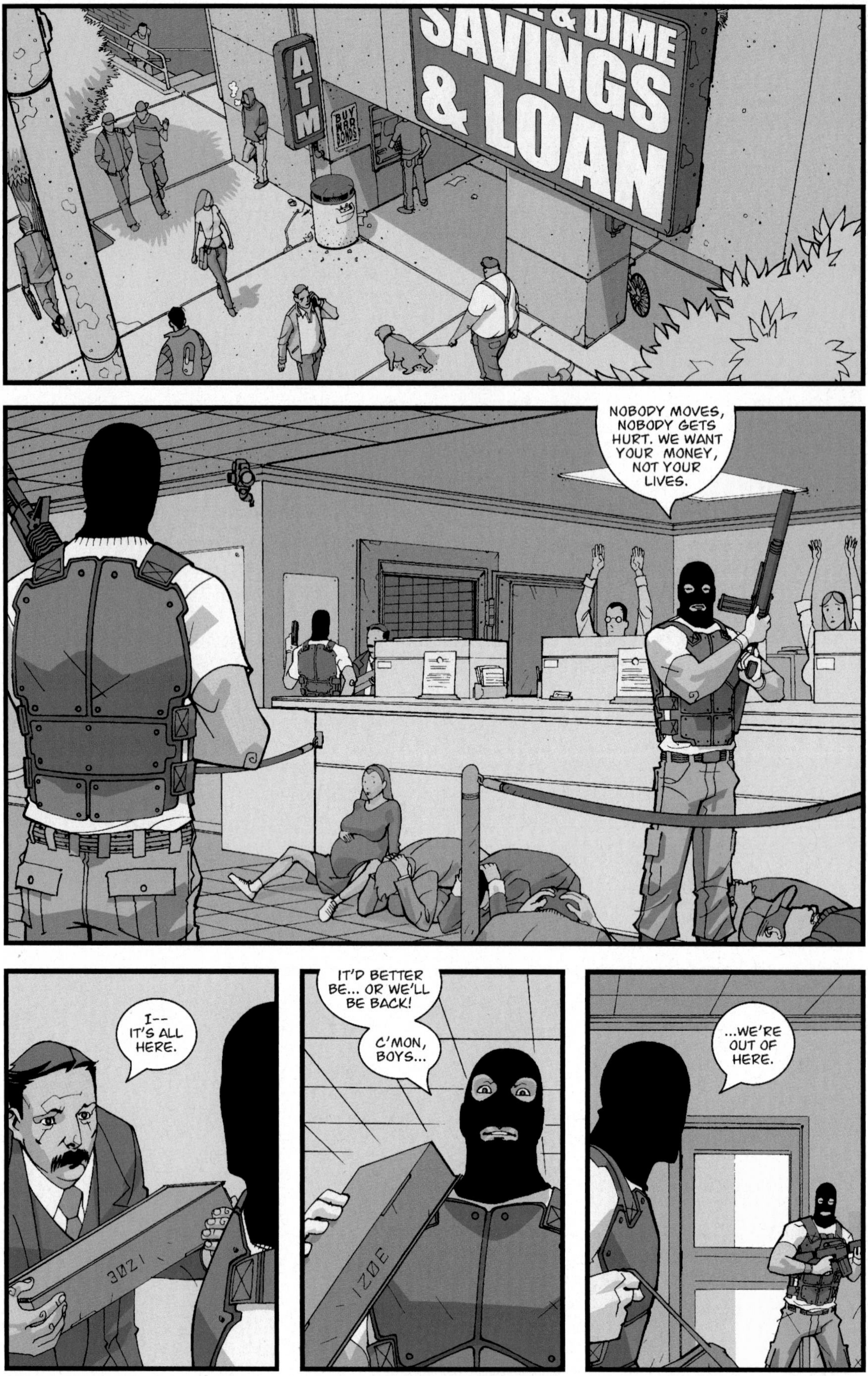
SAVINGS & LOAN
ATM
BUY WAR BONDS
NOBODY MOVES, NOBODY GETS HURT. WE WANT YOUR MONEY, NOT YOUR LIVES.
I-- IT'S ALL HERE.
IT'D BETTER BE... OR WE'LL BE BACK!
C'MON, BOYS...
...WE'RE OUT OF HERE.

CHAPTER TWO

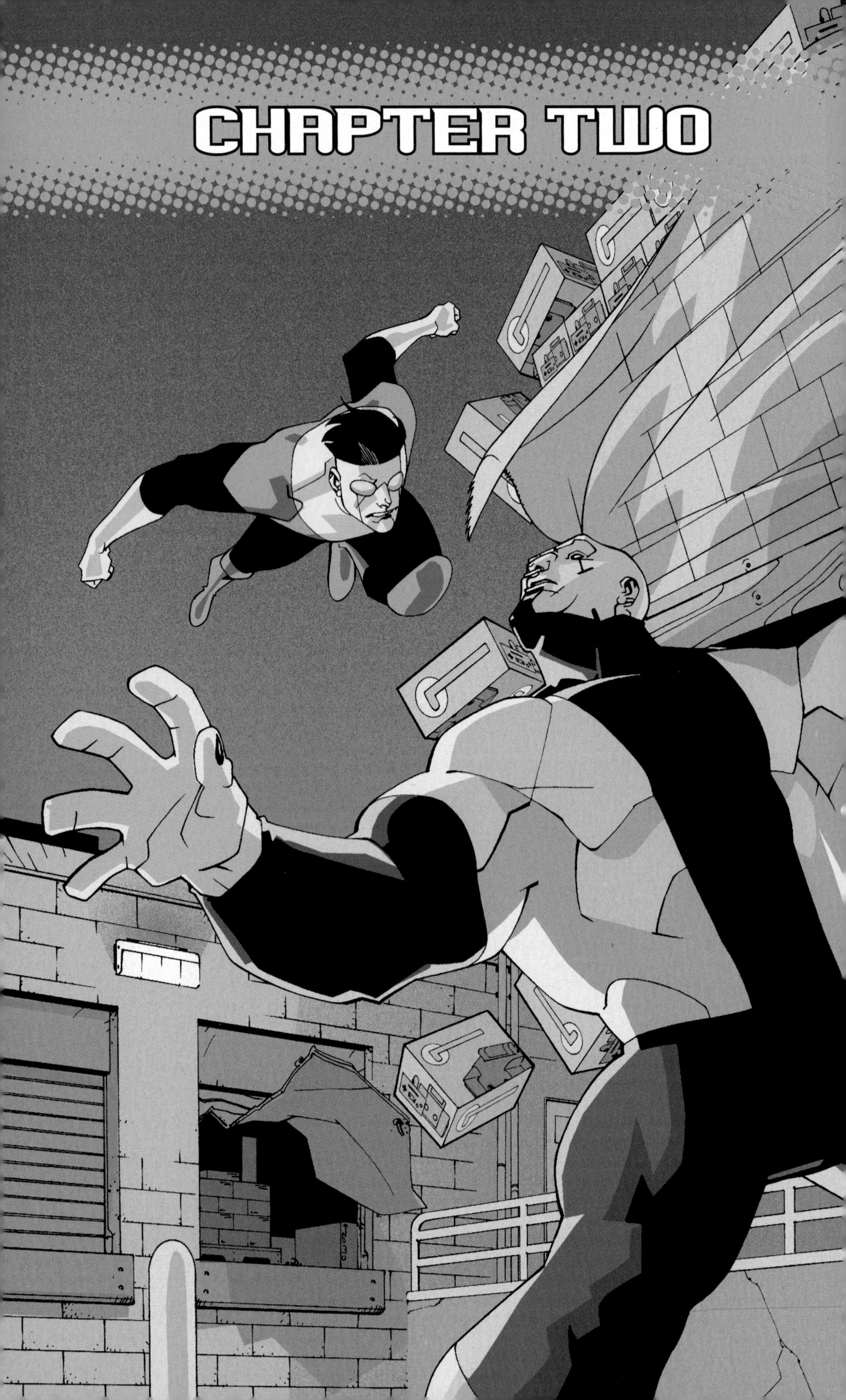

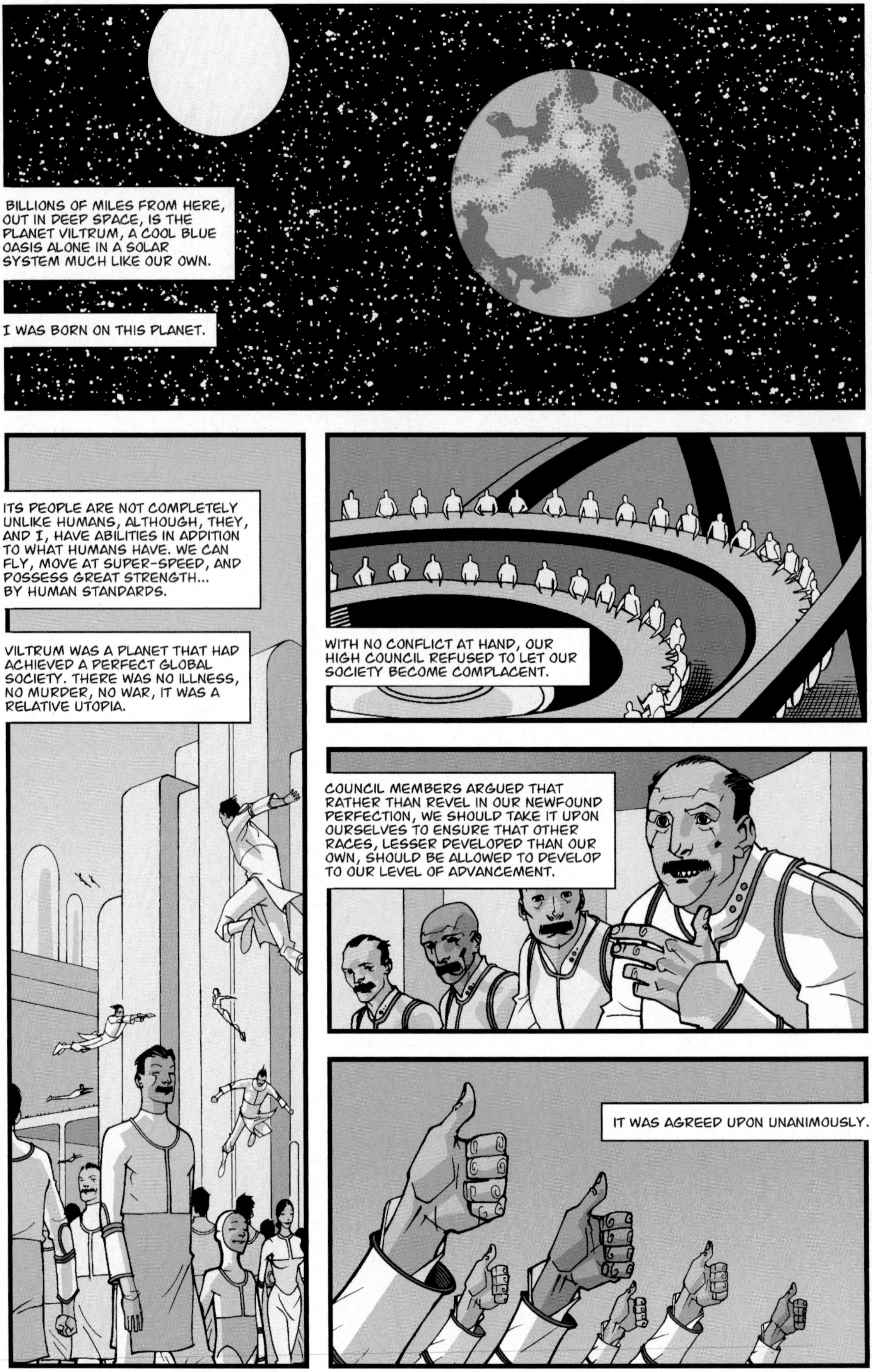
BILLIONS OF MILES FROM HERE, OUT IN DEEP SPACE, IS THE PLANET VILTRUM, A COOL BLUE OASIS ALONE IN A SOLAR SYSTEM MUCH LIKE OUR OWN.
I WAS BORN ON THIS PLANET.
ITS PEOPLE ARE NOT COMPLETELY UNLIKE HUMANS, ALTHOUGH, THEY, AND I, HAVE ABILITIES IN ADDITION TO WHAT HUMANS HAVE. WE CAN FLY, MOVE AT SUPER-SPEED, AND POSSESS GREAT STRENGTH... BY HUMAN STANDARDS.
VILTRUM WAS A PLANET THAT HAD ACHIEVED A PERFECT GLOBAL SOCIETY. THERE WAS NO ILLNESS, NO MURDER, NO WAR, IT WAS A RELATIVE UTOPIA.
WITH NO CONFLICT AT HAND, OUR HIGH COUNCIL REFUSED TO LET OUR SOCIETY BECOME COMPLACENT.
COUNCIL MEMBERS ARGUED THAT RATHER THAN REVEL IN OUR NEWFOUND PERFECTION, WE SHOULD TAKE IT UPON OURSELVES TO ENSURE THAT OTHER RACES, LESSER DEVELOPED THAN OUR OWN, SHOULD BE ALLOWED TO DEVELOP TO OUR LEVEL OF ADVANCEMENT.
IT WAS AGREED UPON UNANIMOUSLY.

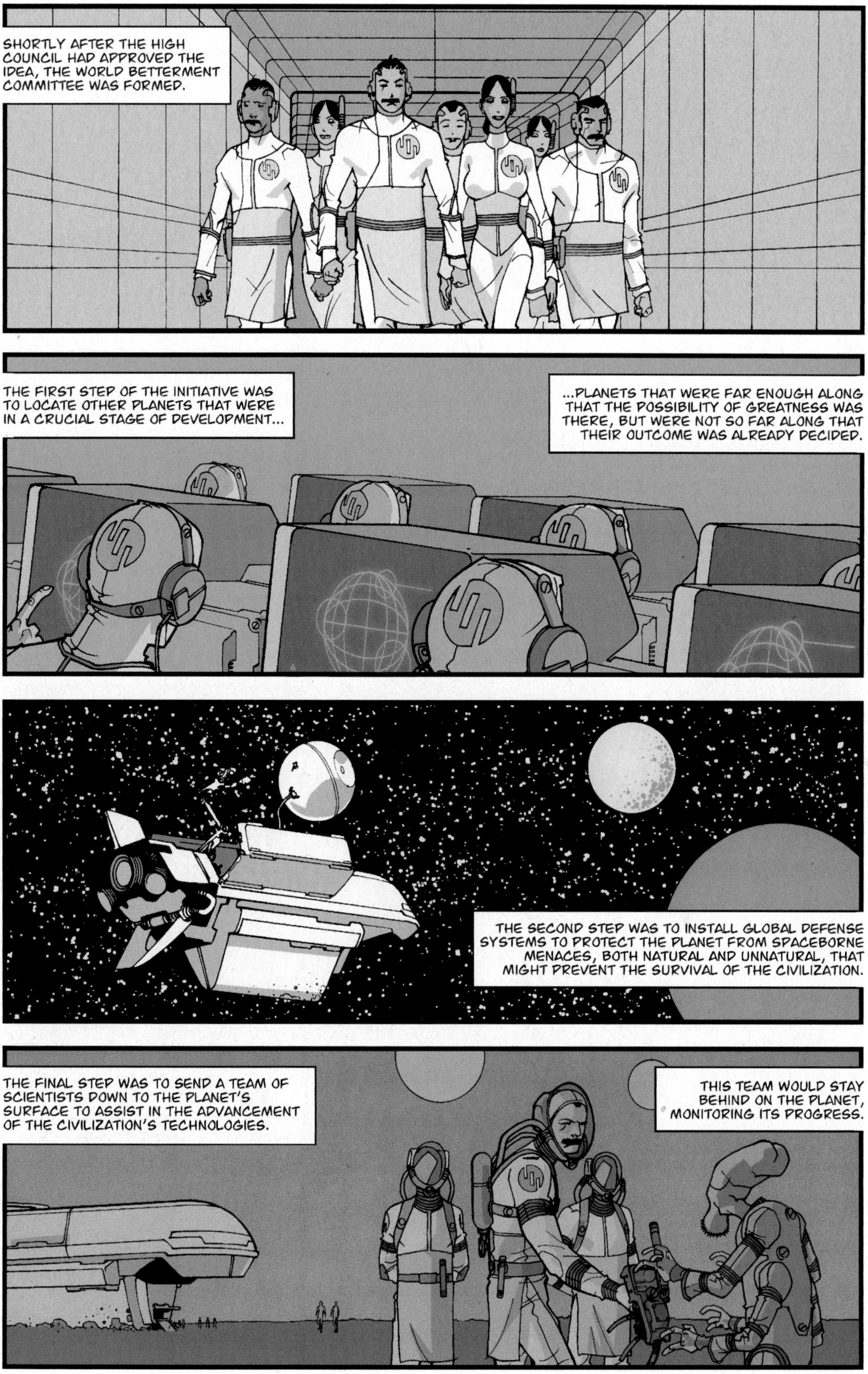
SHORTLY AFTER THE HIGH COUNCIL HAD APPROVED THE IDEA, THE WORLD BETTERMENT COMMITTEE WAS FORMED.
THE FIRST STEP OF THE INITIATIVE WAS TO LOCATE OTHER PLANETS THAT WERE IN A CRUCIAL STAGE OF DEVELOPMENT...
...PLANETS THAT WERE FAR ENOUGH ALONG THAT THE POSSIBILITY OF GREATNESS WAS THERE, BUT WERE NOT SO FAR ALONG THAT THEIR OUTCOME WAS ALREADY DECIDED.
THE SECOND STEP WAS TO INSTALL GLOBAL DEFENSE SYSTEMS TO PROTECT THE PLANET FROM SPACEBORNE MENACES, BOTH NATURAL AND UNNATURAL, THAT MIGHT PREVENT THE SURVIVAL OF THE CIVILIZATION.
THE FINAL STEP WAS TO SEND A TEAM OF SCIENTISTS DOWN TO THE PLANET'S SURFACE TO ASSIST IN THE ADVANCEMENT OF THE CIVILIZATION'S TECHNOLOGIES.
THIS TEAM WOULD STAY BEHIND ON THE PLANET, MONITORING ITS PROGRESS.

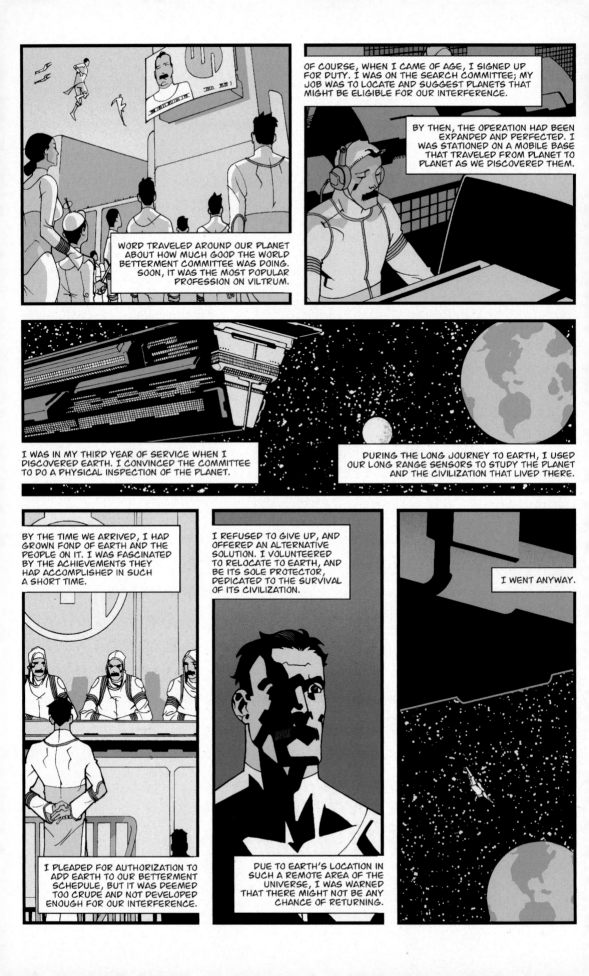

OF COURSE, WHEN I CAME OF AGE, I SIGNED UP FOR DUTY. I WAS ON THE SEARCH COMMITTEE; MY JOB WAS TO LOCATE AND SUGGEST PLANETS THAT MIGHT BE ELIGIBLE FOR OUR INTERFERENCE.

BY THEN, THE OPERATION HAD BEEN EXPANDED AND PERFECTED. I WAS STATIONED ON A MOBILE BASE THAT TRAVELED FROM PLANET TO PLANET AS WE DISCOVERED THEM.

WORD TRAVELED AROUND OUR PLANET ABOUT HOW MUCH GOOD THE WORLD BETTERMENT COMMITTEE WAS DOING. SOON, IT WAS THE MOST POPULAR PROFESSION ON VILTRUM.

I WAS IN MY THIRD YEAR OF SERVICE WHEN I DISCOVERED EARTH. I CONVINCED THE COMMITTEE TO DO A PHYSICAL INSPECTION OF THE PLANET.

DURING THE LONG JOURNEY TO EARTH, I USED OUR LONG RANGE SENSORS TO STUDY THE PLANET AND THE CIVILIZATION THAT LIVED THERE.

BY THE TIME WE ARRIVED, I HAD GROWN FOND OF EARTH AND THE PEOPLE ON IT. I WAS FASCINATED BY THE ACHIEVEMENTS THEY HAD ACCOMPLISHED IN SUCH A SHORT TIME.

I REFUSED TO GIVE UP, AND OFFERED AN ALTERNATIVE SOLUTION. I VOLUNTEERED TO RELOCATE TO EARTH, AND BE ITS SOLE PROTECTOR, DEDICATED TO THE SURVIVAL OF ITS CIVILIZATION.

I WENT ANYWAY.

I PLEADED FOR AUTHORIZATION TO ADD EARTH TO OUR BETTERMENT SCHEDULE, BUT IT WAS DEEMED TOO CRUDE AND NOT DEVELOPED ENOUGH FOR OUR INTERFERENCE.

DUE TO EARTH'S LOCATION IN SUCH A REMOTE AREA OF THE UNIVERSE, I WAS WARNED THAT THERE MIGHT NOT BE ANY CHANCE OF RETURNING.

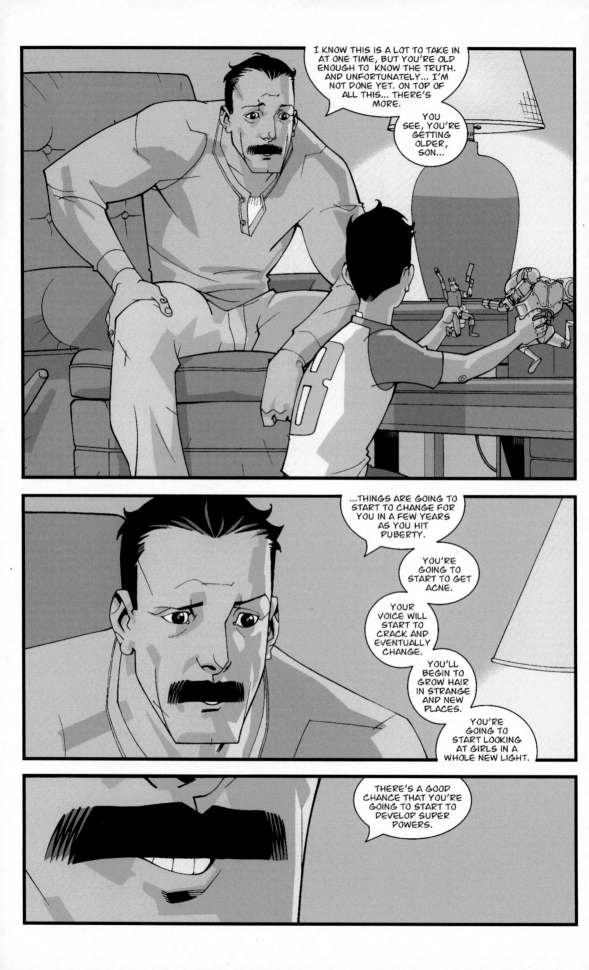

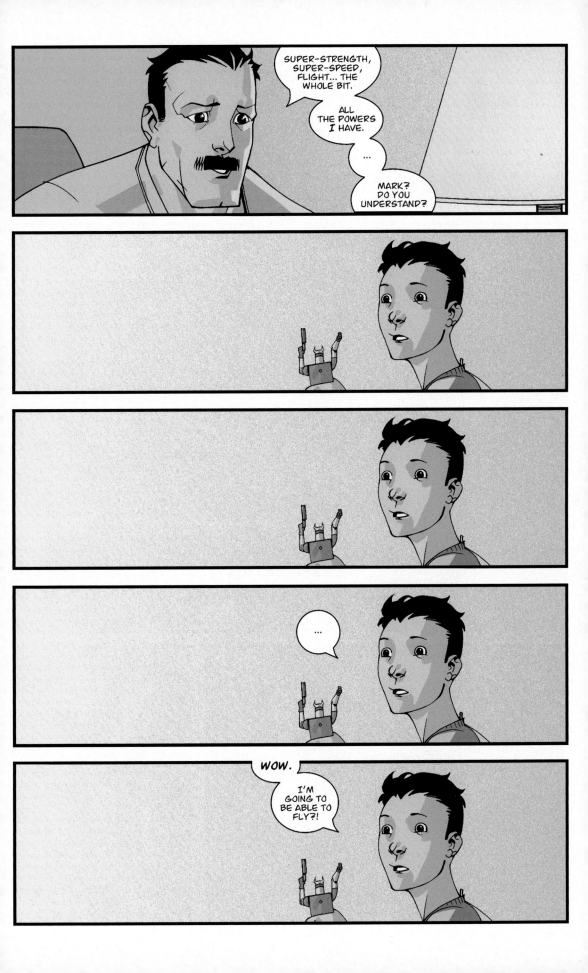

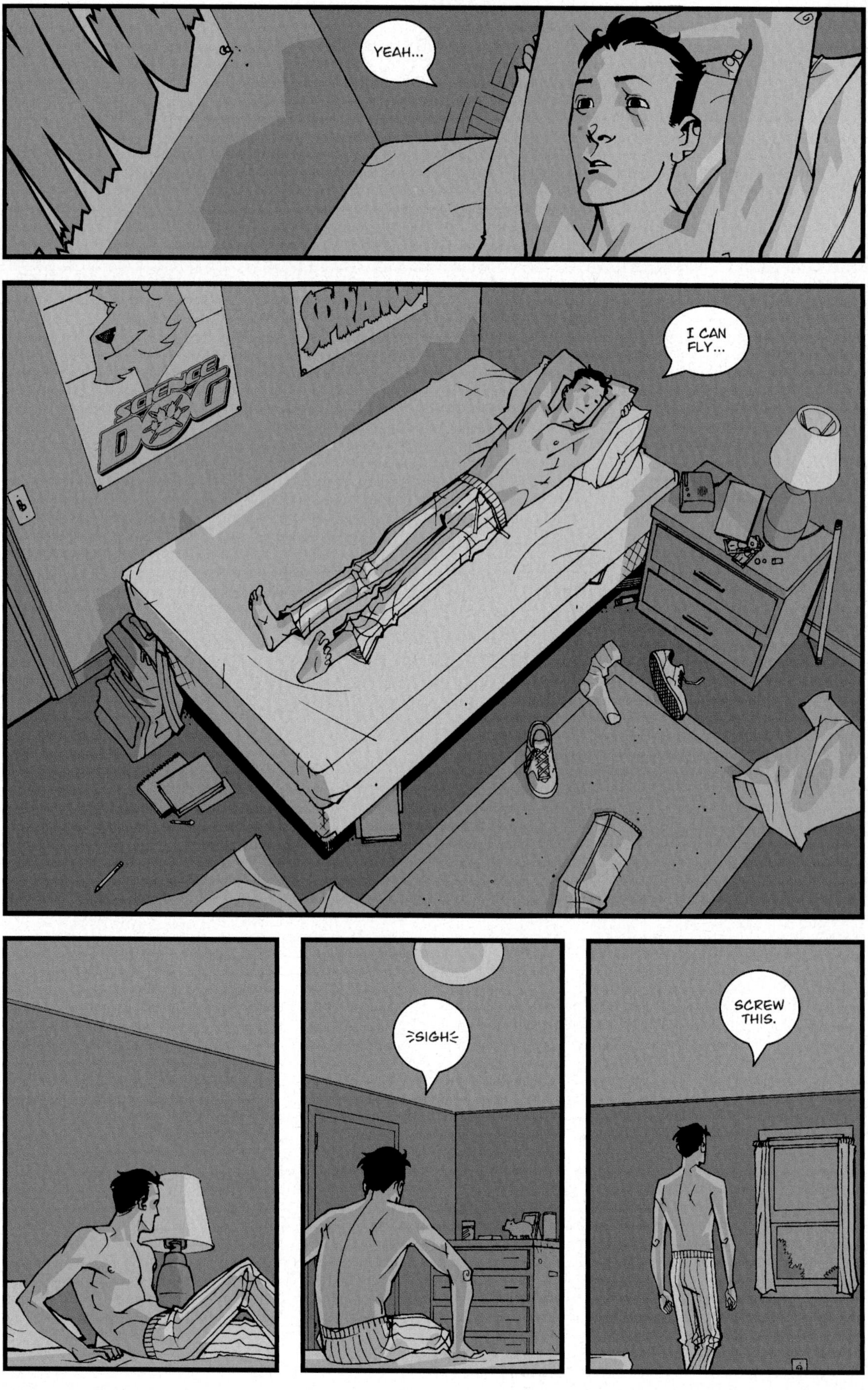
YEAH...
SCIENCE DOG
I CAN FLY...
SIGH
SCREW THIS.

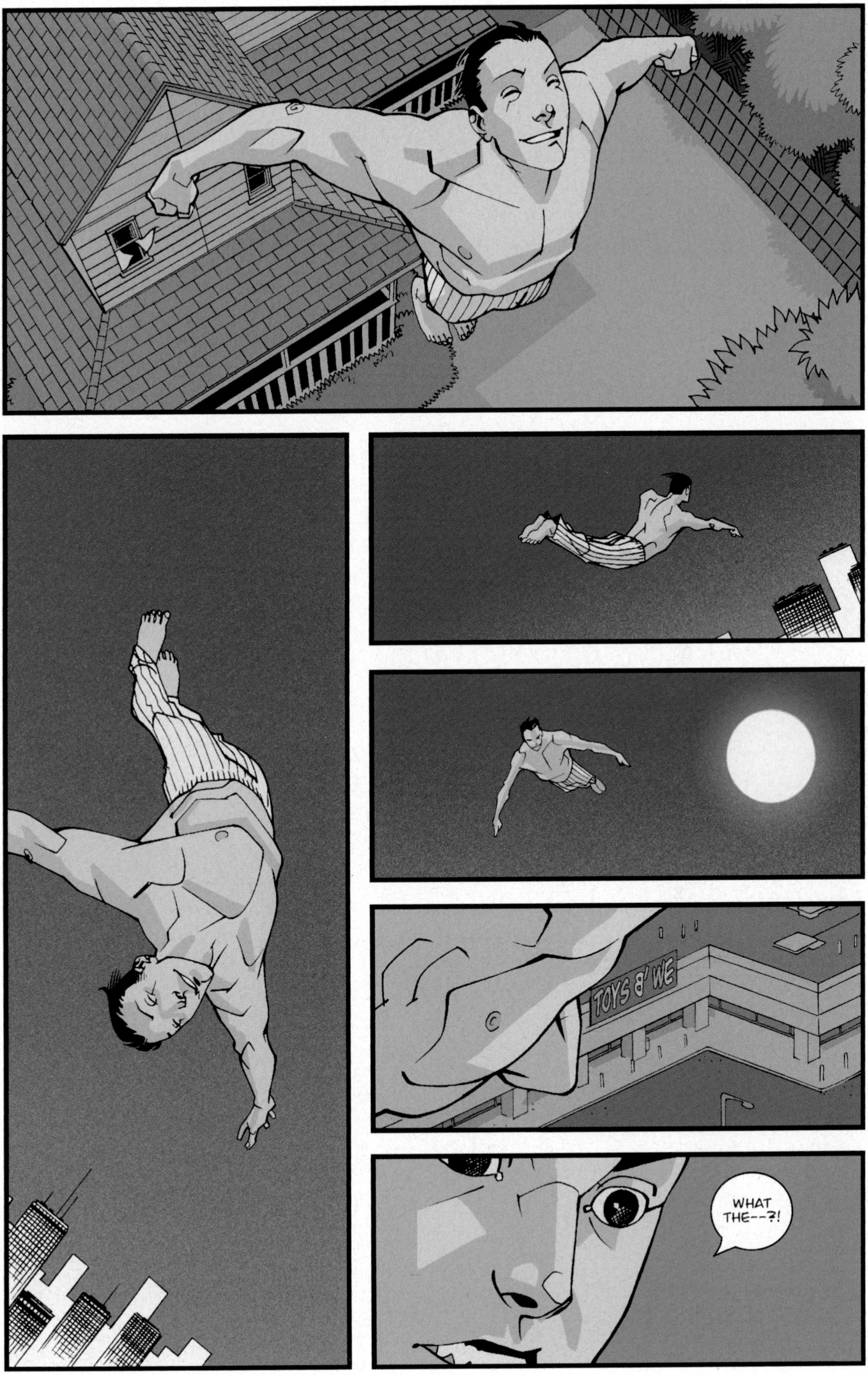
TOYS 8' WE
WHAT THE--?!

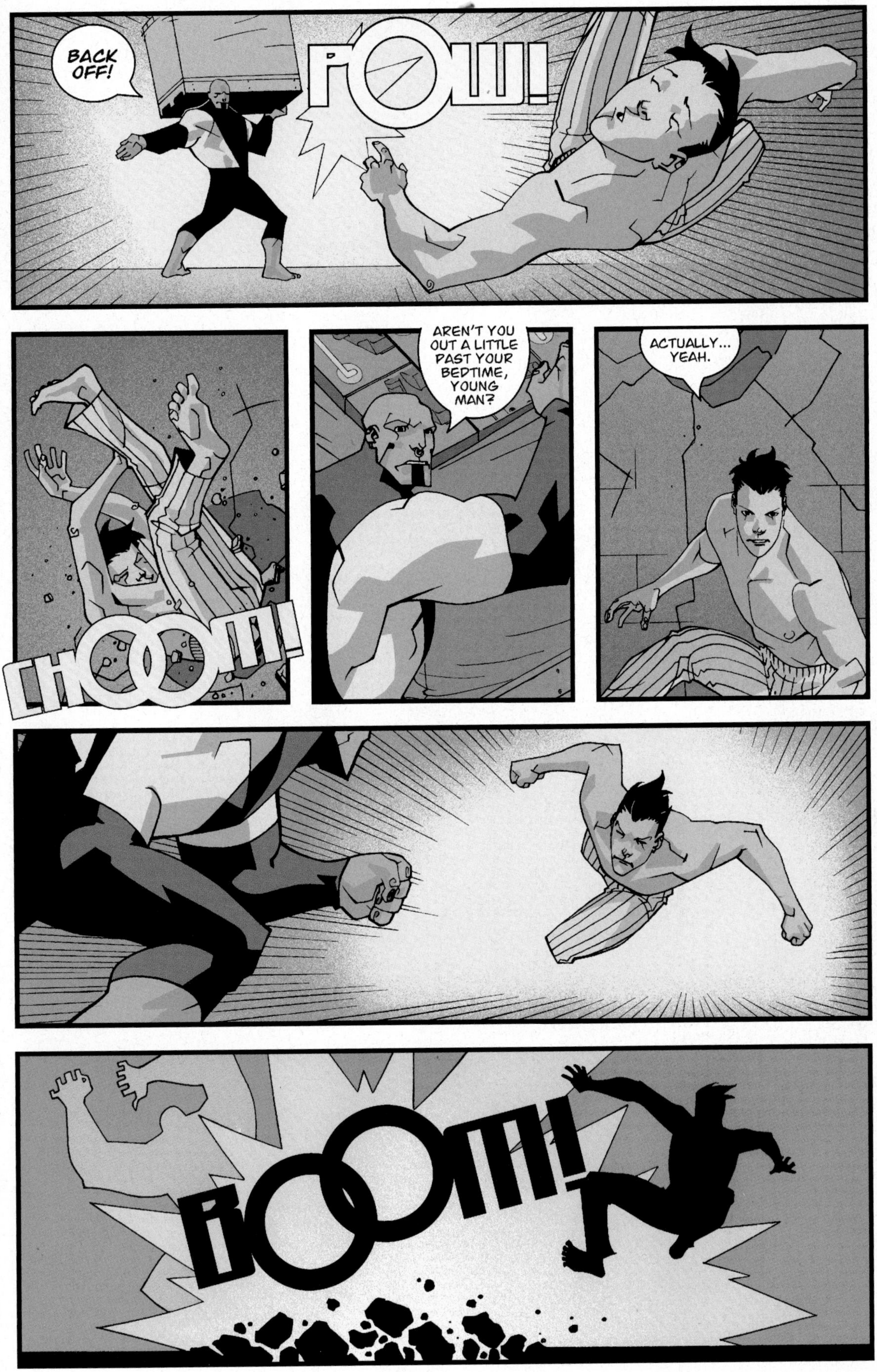
BACK OFF!
POW!
CHOOM!
AREN'T YOU OUT A LITTLE PAST YOUR BEDTIME, YOUNG MAN?
ACTUALLY... YEAH.
BOOM!

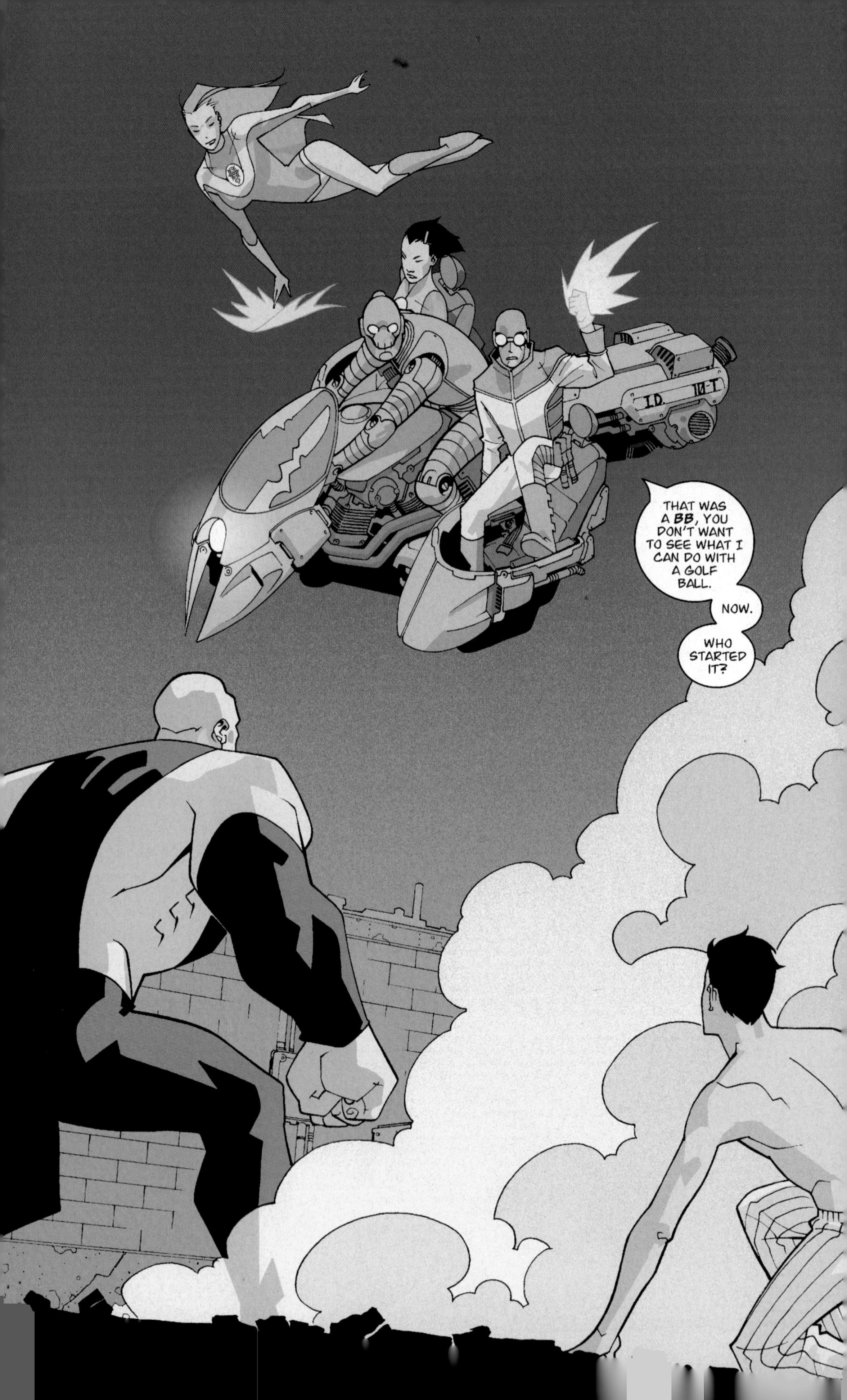
I.D. 10-T
THAT WAS A BB, YOU DON'T WANT TO SEE WHAT I CAN DO WITH A GOLF BALL.
NOW.
WHO STARTED IT?

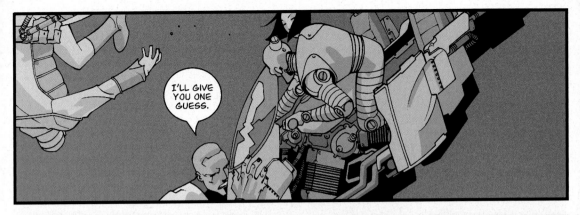

I'LL GIVE YOU ONE GUESS.

SKRA-GOOOM!

WAY TO GO, REX. WE *HAD* THE ELEMENT OF SURPRISE.

SORRY, 'BOT. IT SEEMED LIKE A GOOD IDEA AT THE TIME.

WELL, TRY TO LEAVE THE GOOD IDEAS UP TO ME.

AND, UM...

...WE'RE GOING TO NEED ONE REAL SOON.

YOU GOT THAT RIGHT!

KRAK!

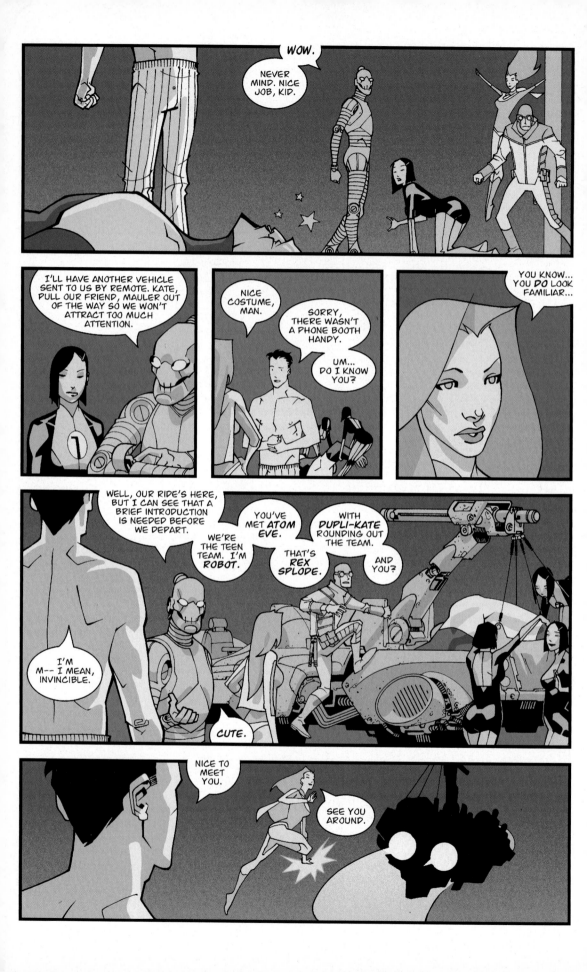

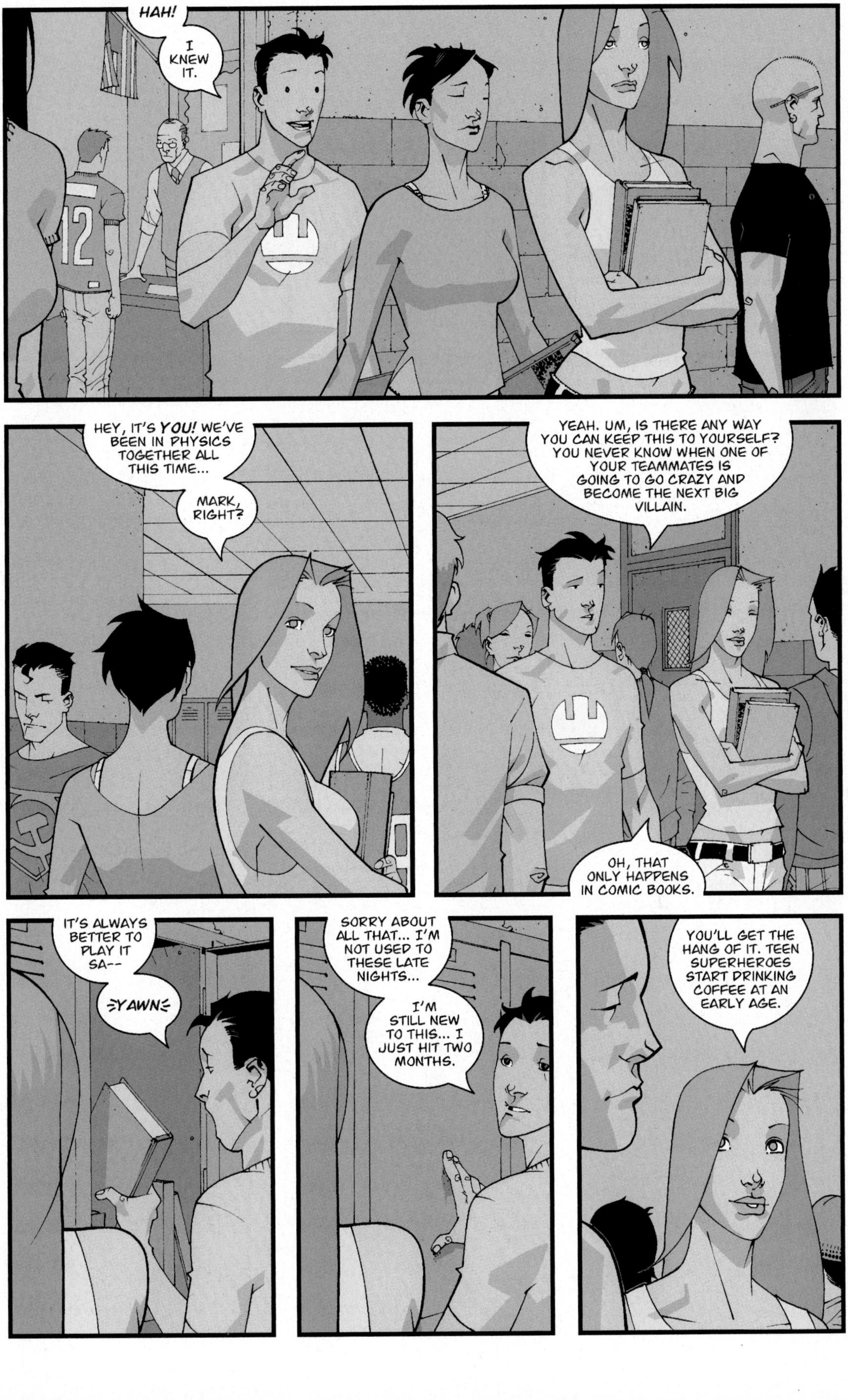
HAH!
I KNEW IT.
HEY, IT'S *YOU!* WE'VE BEEN IN PHYSICS TOGETHER ALL THIS TIME...
MARK, RIGHT?
YEAH. UM, IS THERE ANY WAY YOU CAN KEEP THIS TO YOURSELF? YOU NEVER KNOW WHEN ONE OF YOUR TEAMMATES IS GOING TO GO CRAZY AND BECOME THE NEXT BIG VILLAIN.
OH, THAT ONLY HAPPENS IN COMIC BOOKS.
IT'S ALWAYS BETTER TO PLAY IT SA--
YAWN
SORRY ABOUT ALL THAT... I'M NOT USED TO THESE LATE NIGHTS...
I'M STILL NEW TO THIS... I JUST HIT TWO MONTHS.
YOU'LL GET THE HANG OF IT. TEEN SUPERHEROES START DRINKING COFFEE AT AN EARLY AGE.

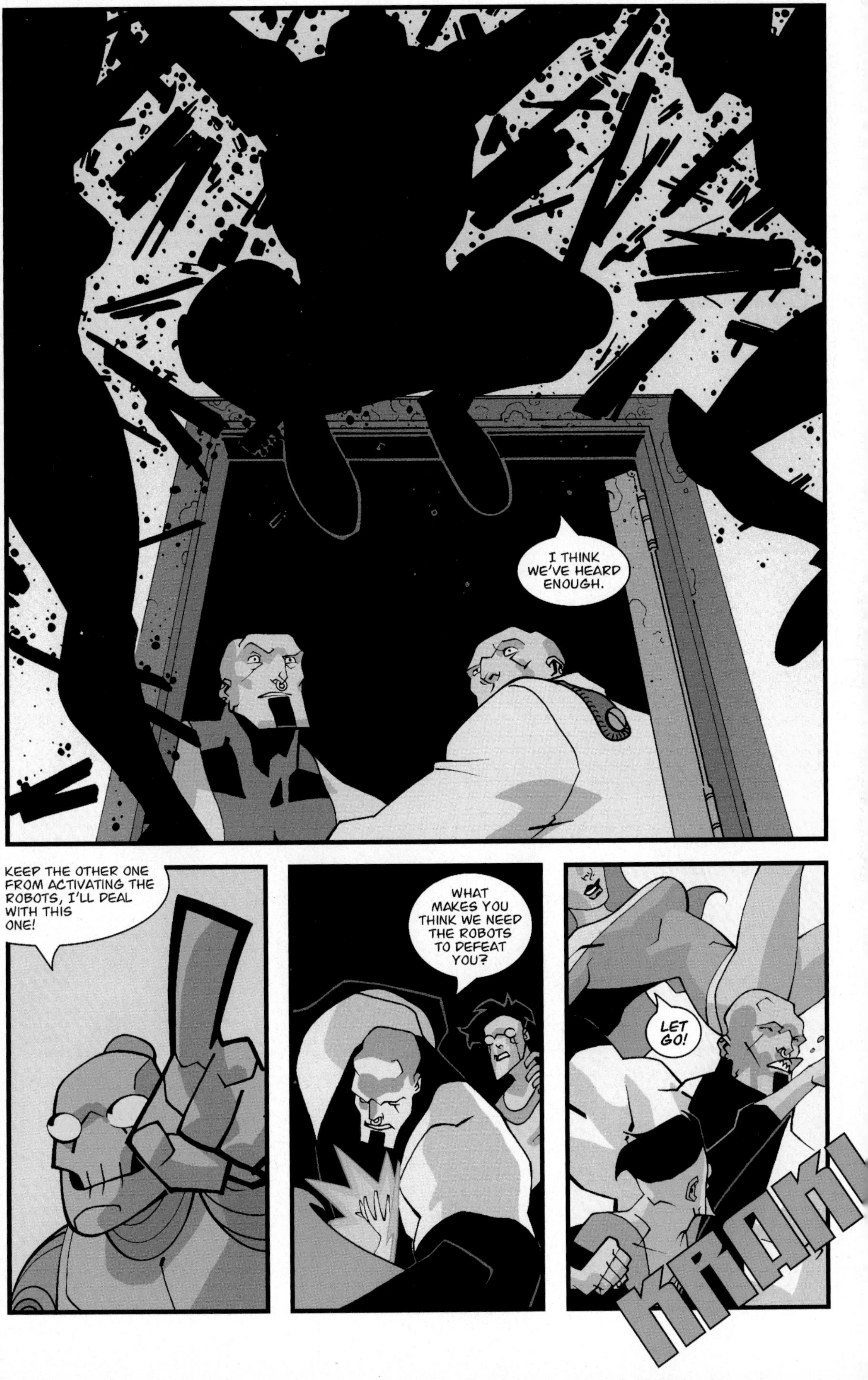
I THINK WE'VE HEARD ENOUGH.
KEEP THE OTHER ONE FROM ACTIVATING THE ROBOTS, I'LL DEAL WITH THIS ONE!
WHAT MAKES YOU THINK WE NEED THE ROBOTS TO DEFEAT YOU?
LET GO!
KRAAK!

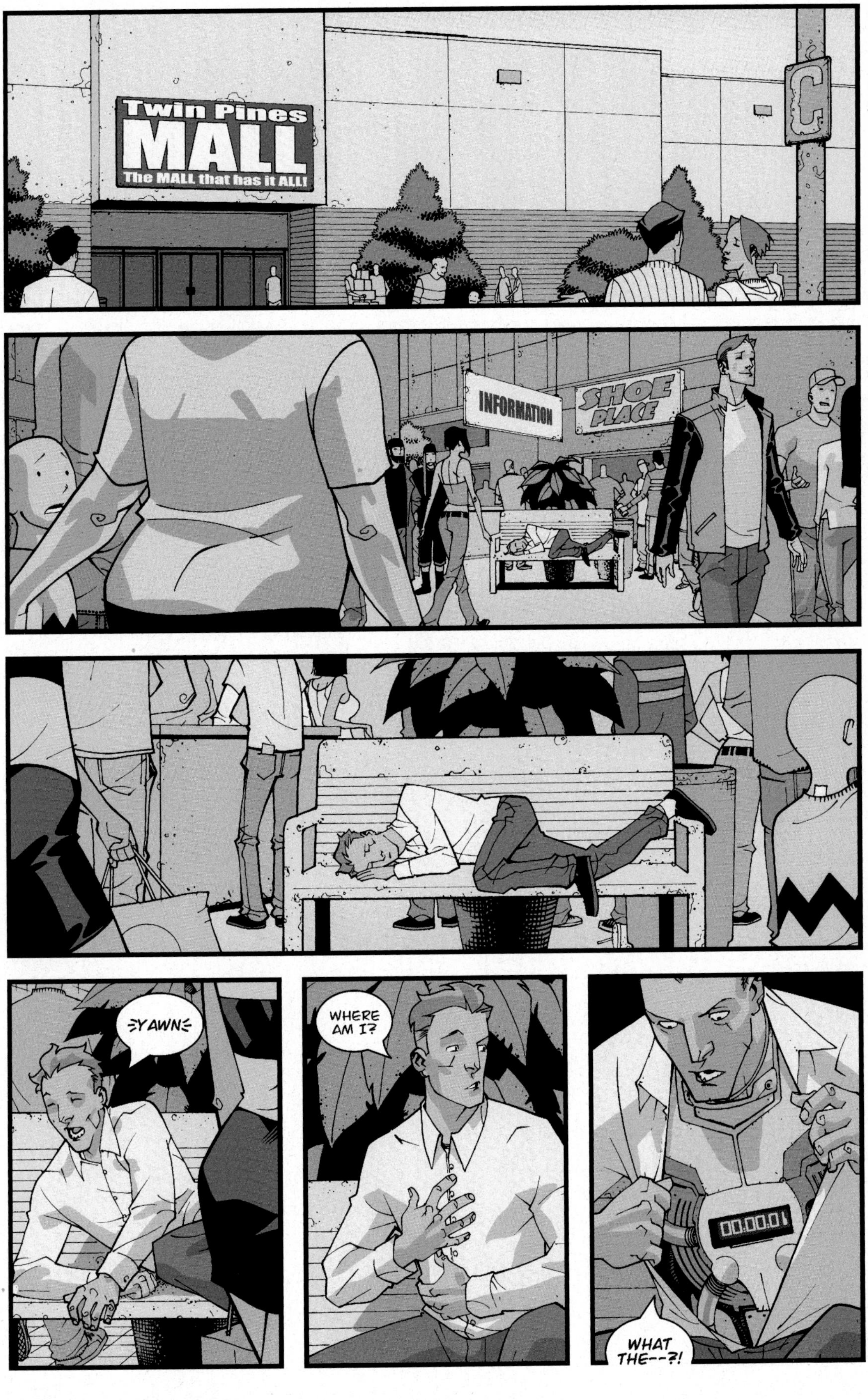
Twin Pines
MALL
The MALL that has it ALL!
C
INFORMATION
SHOE PLACE
YAWN
WHERE AM I?
00.00.01
WHAT THE--?!

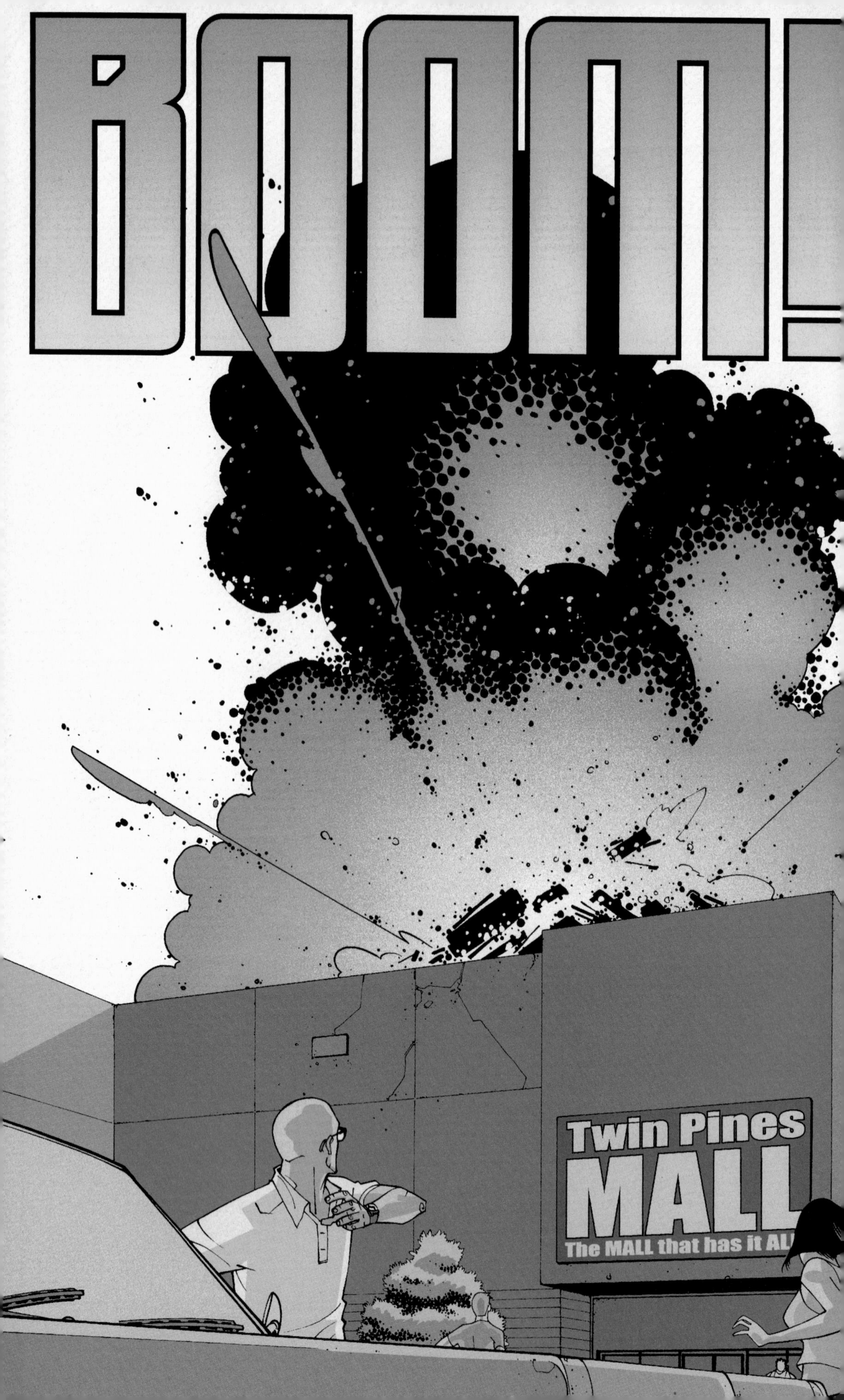
BOOM!
Twin Pines
MALL
The MALL that has it ALL

CHAPTER THREE

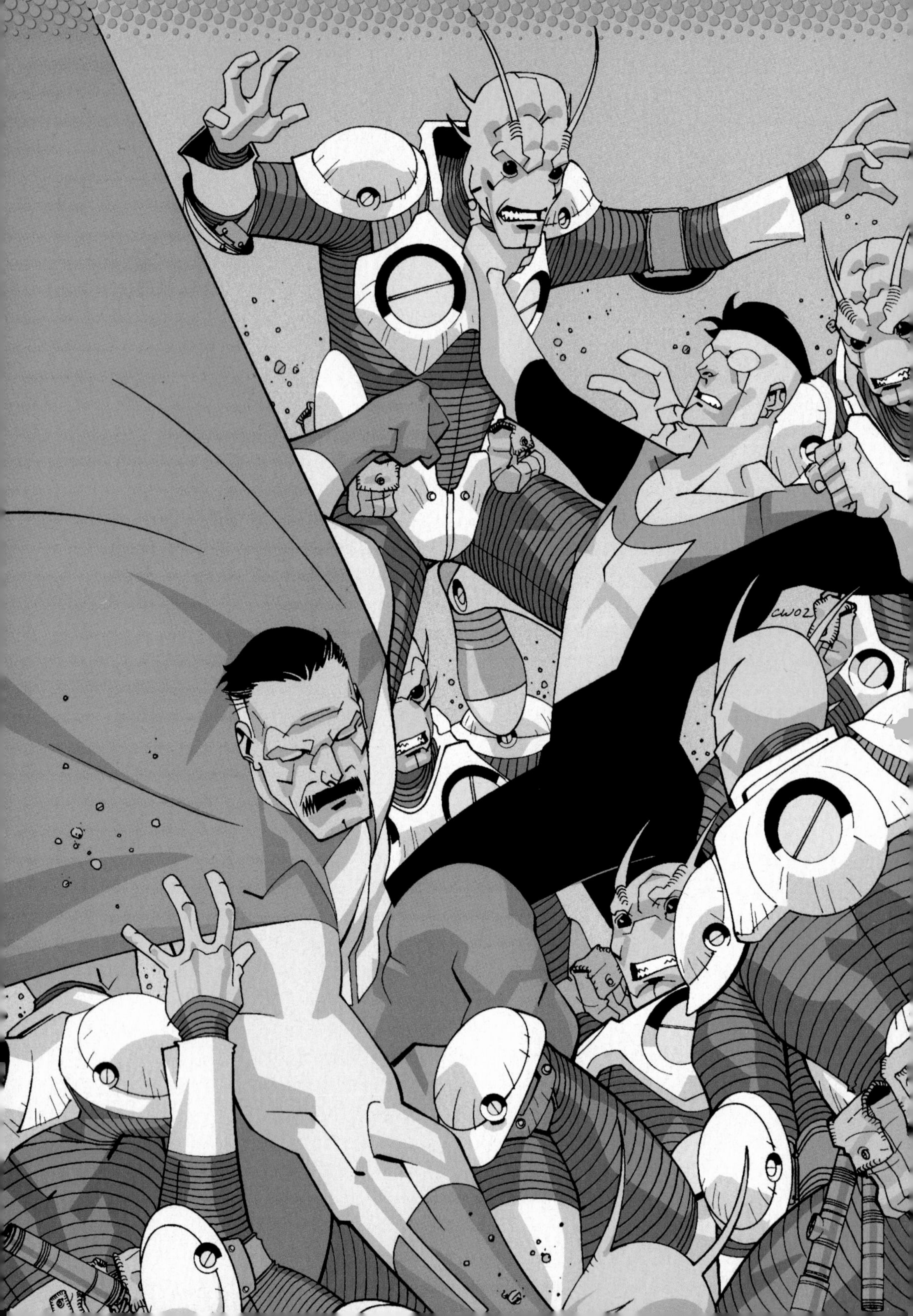
CW02

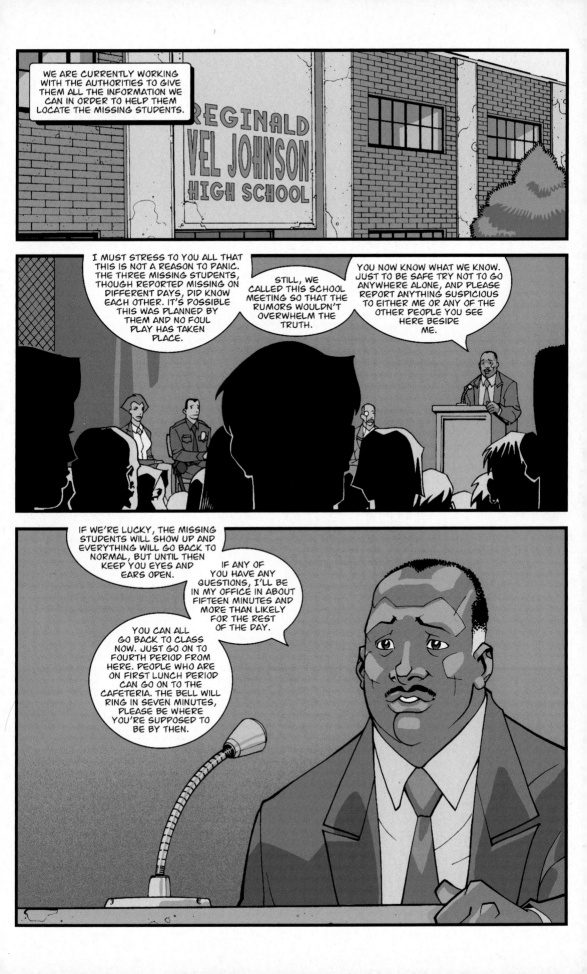

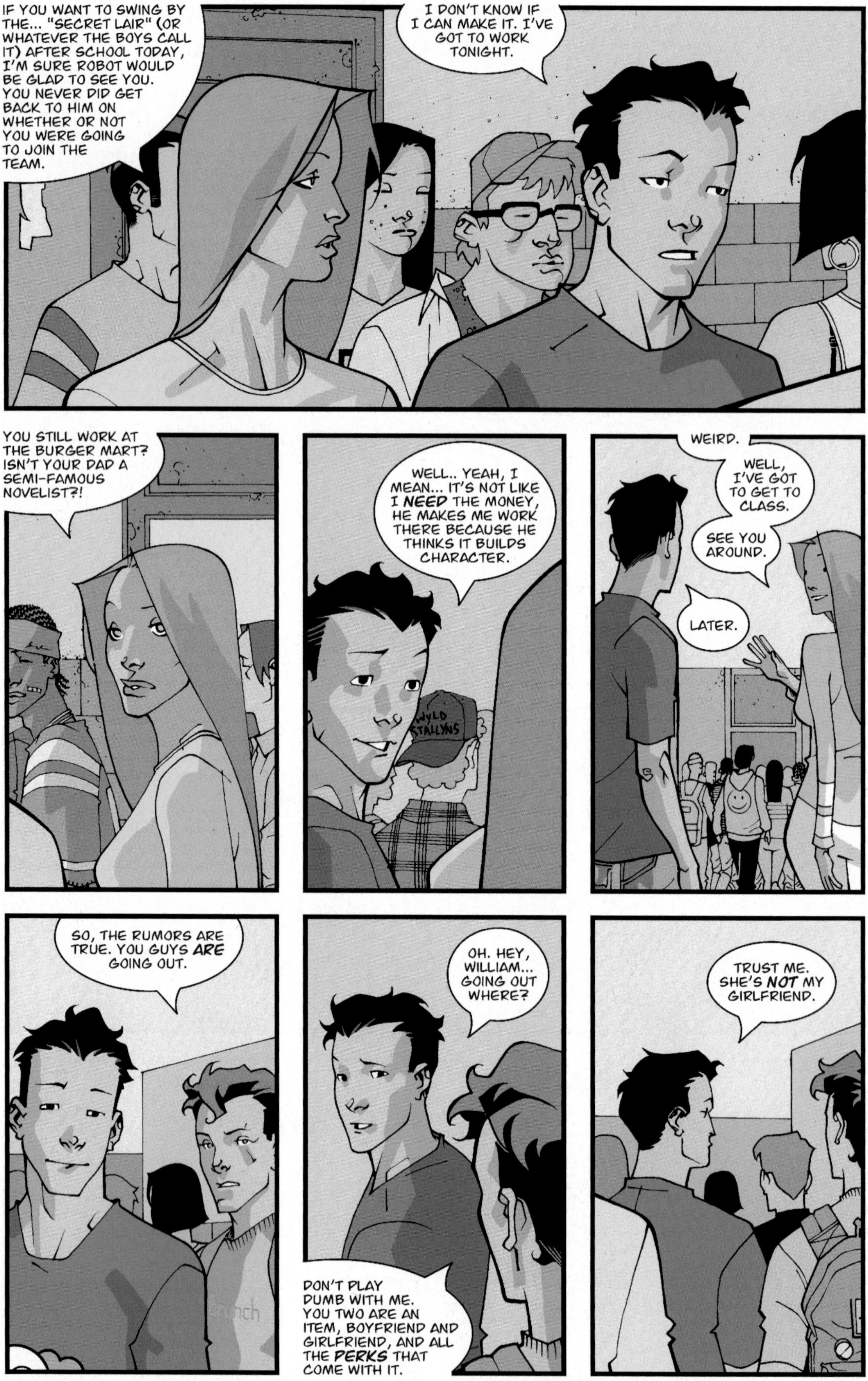
IF YOU WANT TO SWING BY THE... "SECRET LAIR" (OR WHATEVER THE BOYS CALL IT) AFTER SCHOOL TODAY, I'M SURE ROBOT WOULD BE GLAD TO SEE YOU. YOU NEVER DID GET BACK TO HIM ON WHETHER OR NOT YOU WERE GOING TO JOIN THE TEAM.
I DON'T KNOW IF I CAN MAKE IT. I'VE GOT TO WORK TONIGHT.
YOU STILL WORK AT THE BURGER MART? ISN'T YOUR DAD A SEMI-FAMOUS NOVELIST?!
WELL.. YEAH, I MEAN... IT'S NOT LIKE I **NEED** THE MONEY, HE MAKES ME WORK THERE BECAUSE HE THINKS IT BUILDS CHARACTER.
WYLD STALLYNS
WEIRD.
WELL, I'VE GOT TO GET TO CLASS.
SEE YOU AROUND.
LATER.
SO, THE RUMORS ARE TRUE. YOU GUYS **ARE** GOING OUT.
OH. HEY, WILLIAM... GOING OUT WHERE?
DON'T PLAY DUMB WITH ME. YOU TWO ARE AN ITEM, BOYFRIEND AND GIRLFRIEND, AND ALL THE **PERKS** THAT COME WITH IT.
TRUST ME. SHE'S **NOT** MY GIRLFRIEND.

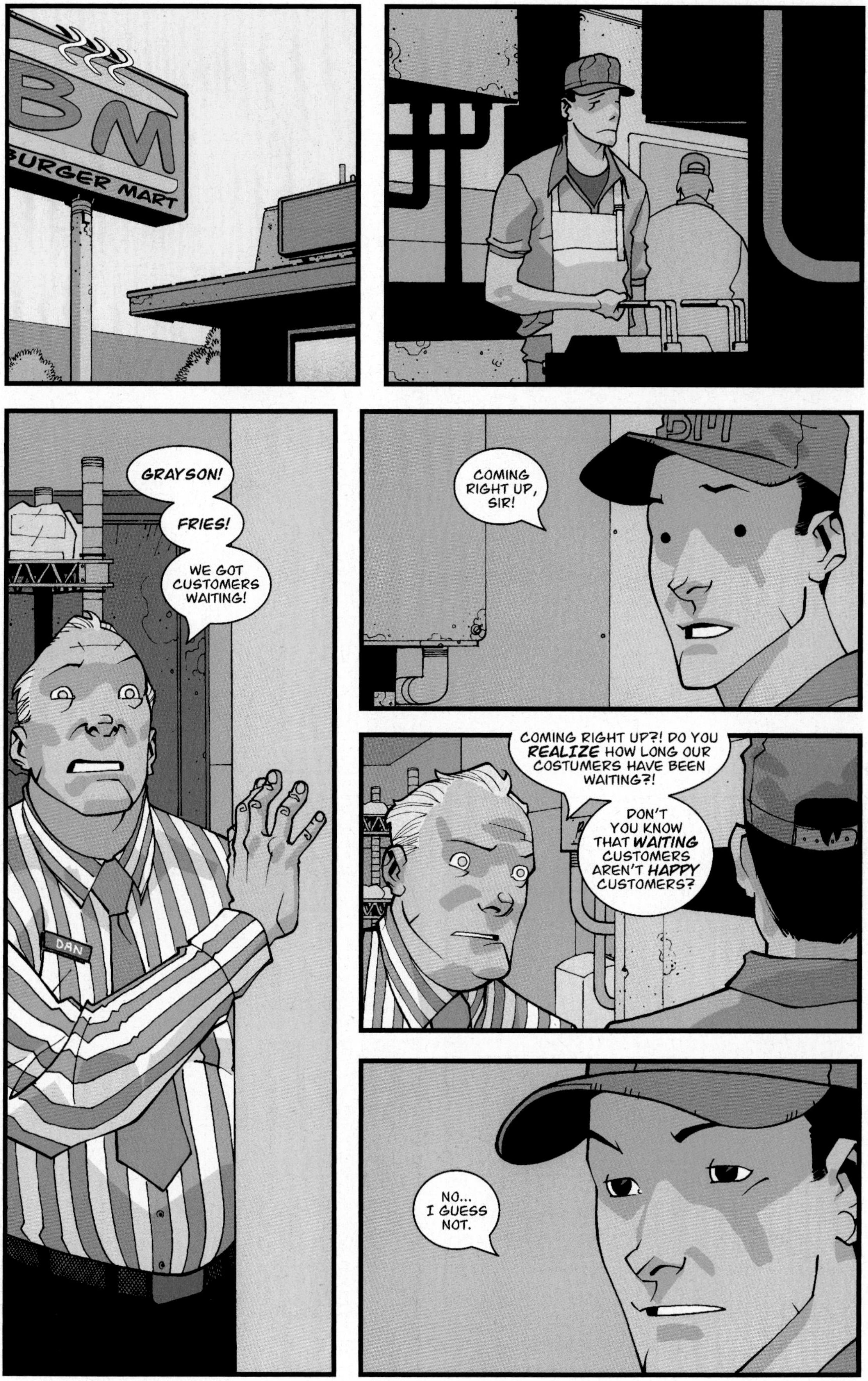
BM
BURGER MART
GRAYSON!
FRIES!
WE GOT CUSTOMERS WAITING!
DAN
COMING RIGHT UP, SIR!
BM
COMING RIGHT UP?! DO YOU REALIZE HOW LONG OUR COSTUMERS HAVE BEEN WAITING?!
DON'T YOU KNOW THAT WAITING CUSTOMERS AREN'T HAPPY CUSTOMERS?
NO... I GUESS NOT.

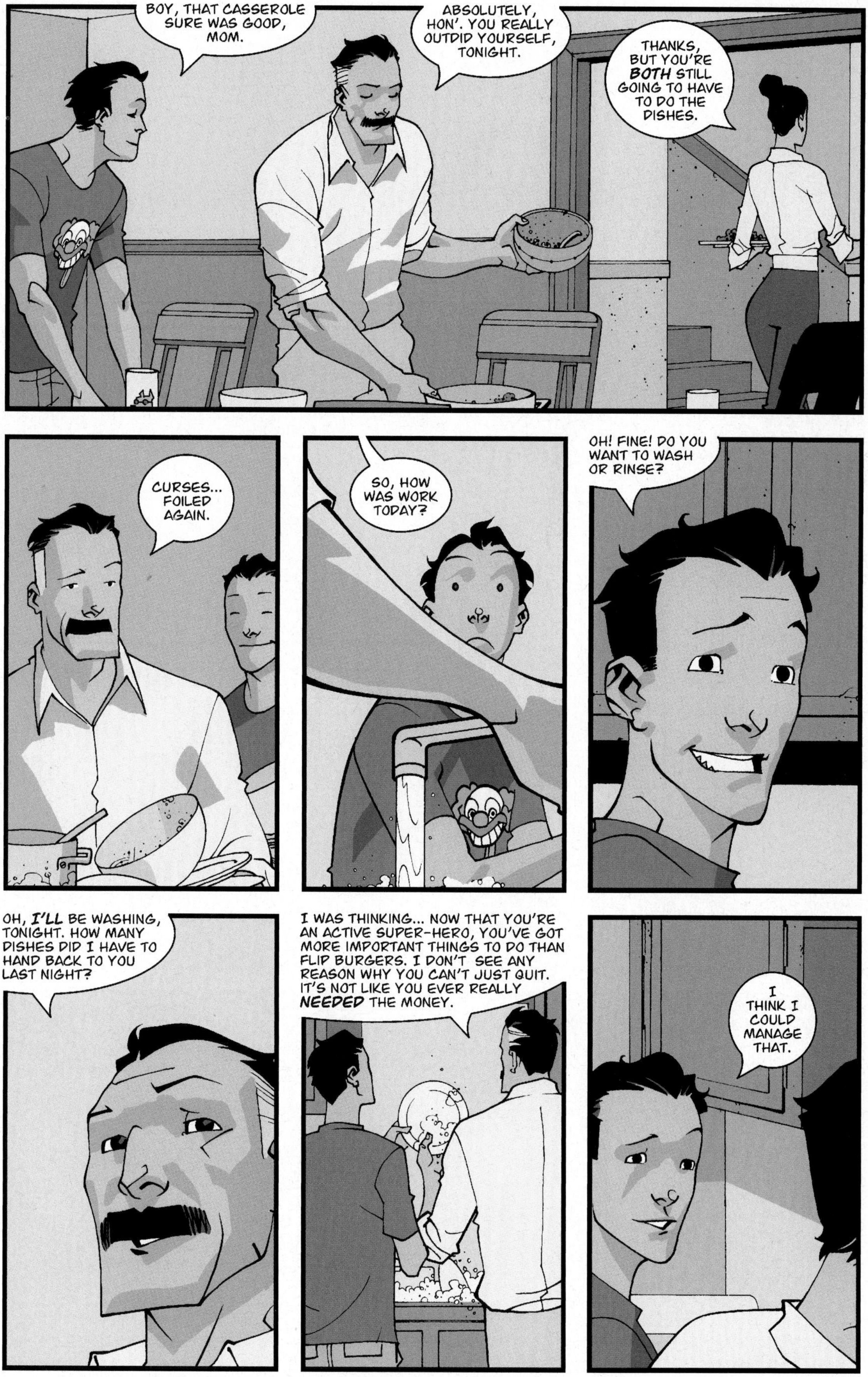
BOY, THAT CASSEROLE SURE WAS GOOD, MOM.
ABSOLUTELY, HON'. YOU REALLY OUTDID YOURSELF, TONIGHT.
THANKS, BUT YOU'RE BOTH STILL GOING TO HAVE TO DO THE DISHES.
CURSES... FOILED AGAIN.
SO, HOW WAS WORK TODAY?
OH! FINE! DO YOU WANT TO WASH OR RINSE?
OH, I'LL BE WASHING, TONIGHT. HOW MANY DISHES DID I HAVE TO HAND BACK TO YOU LAST NIGHT?
I WAS THINKING... NOW THAT YOU'RE AN ACTIVE SUPER-HERO, YOU'VE GOT MORE IMPORTANT THINGS TO DO THAN FLIP BURGERS. I DON'T SEE ANY REASON WHY YOU CAN'T JUST QUIT. IT'S NOT LIKE YOU EVER REALLY NEEDED THE MONEY.
I THINK I COULD MANAGE THAT.

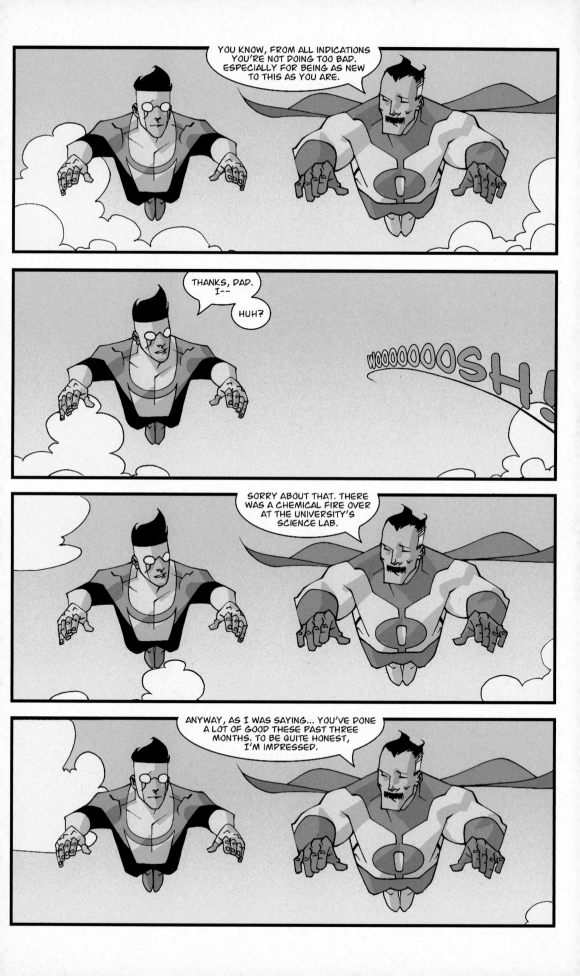

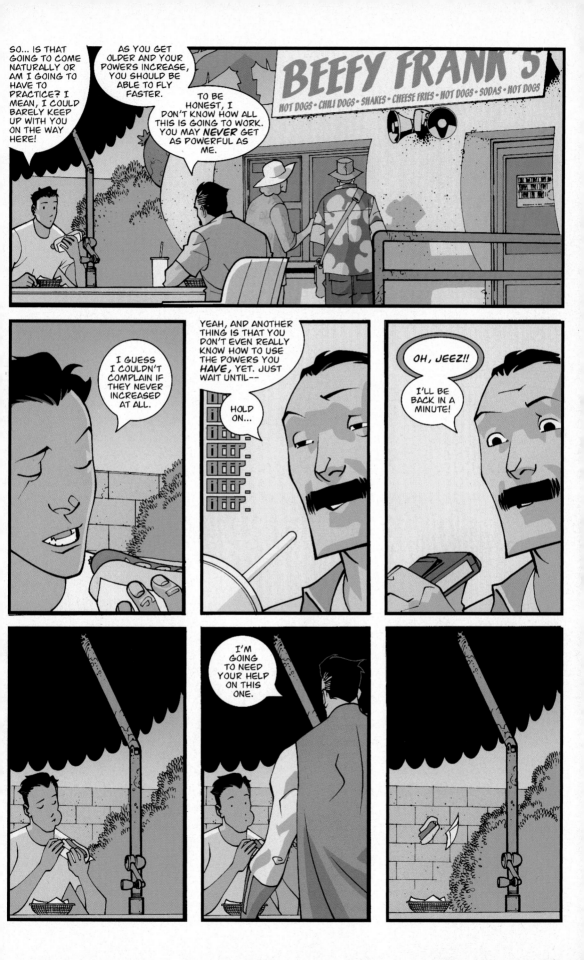

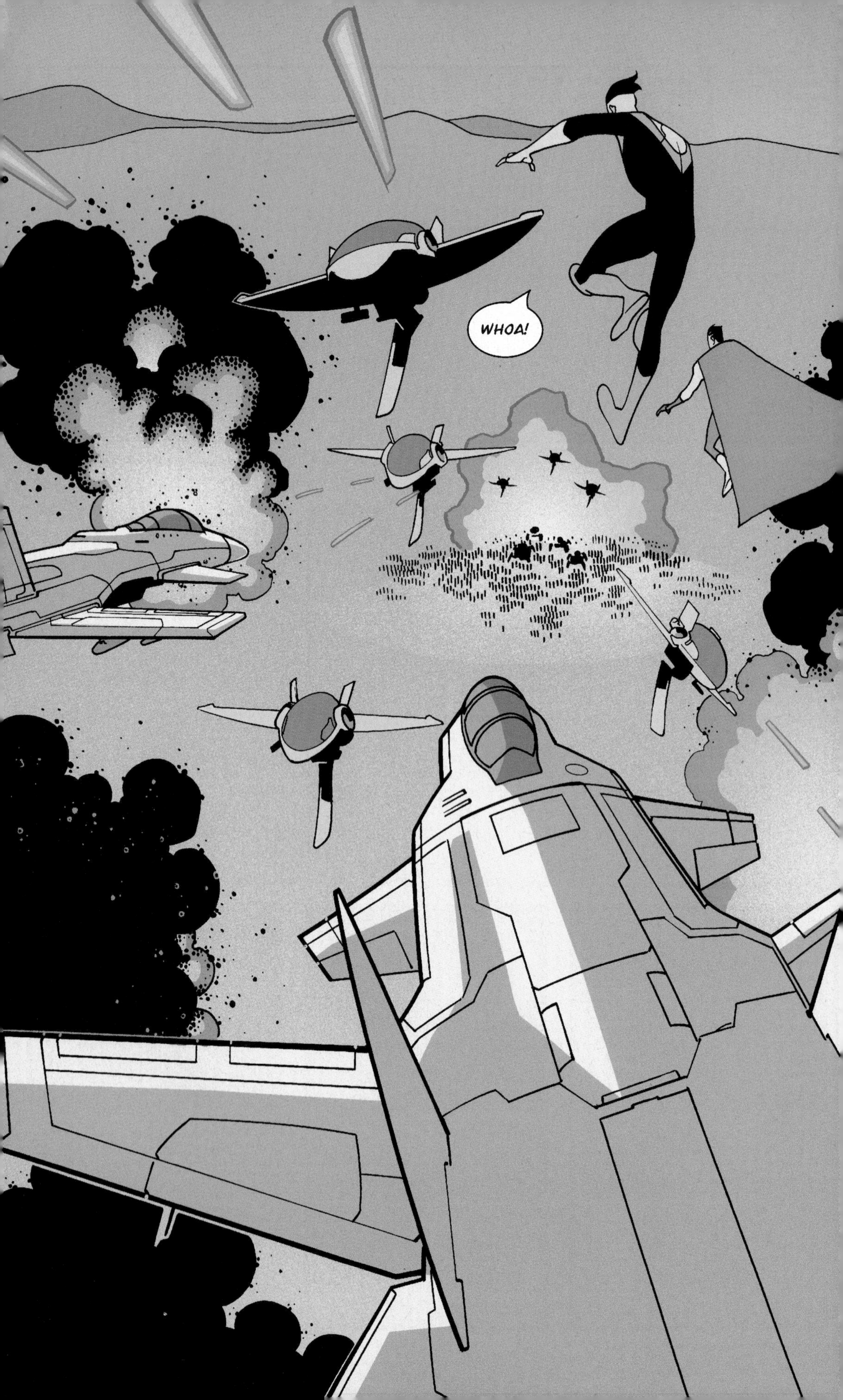
WHOA!

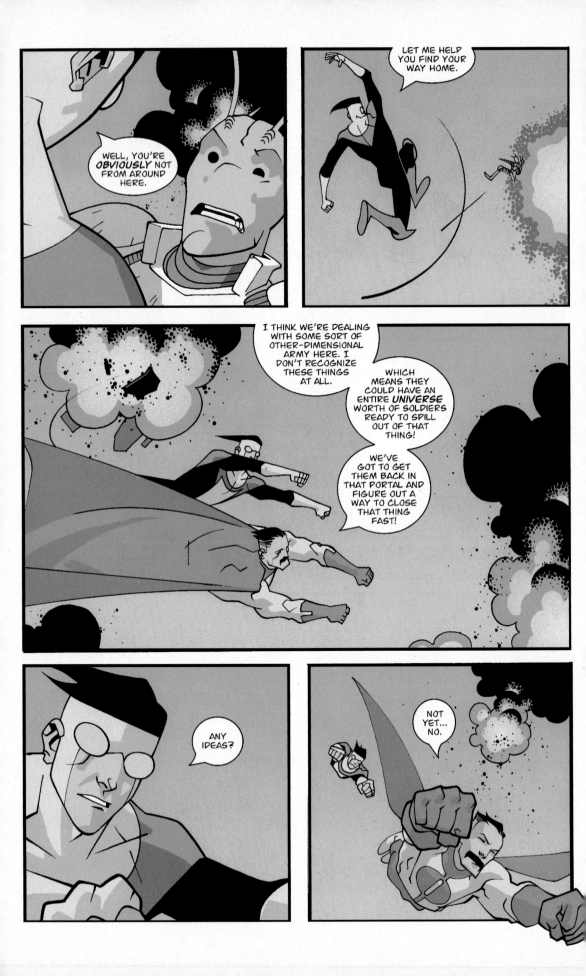

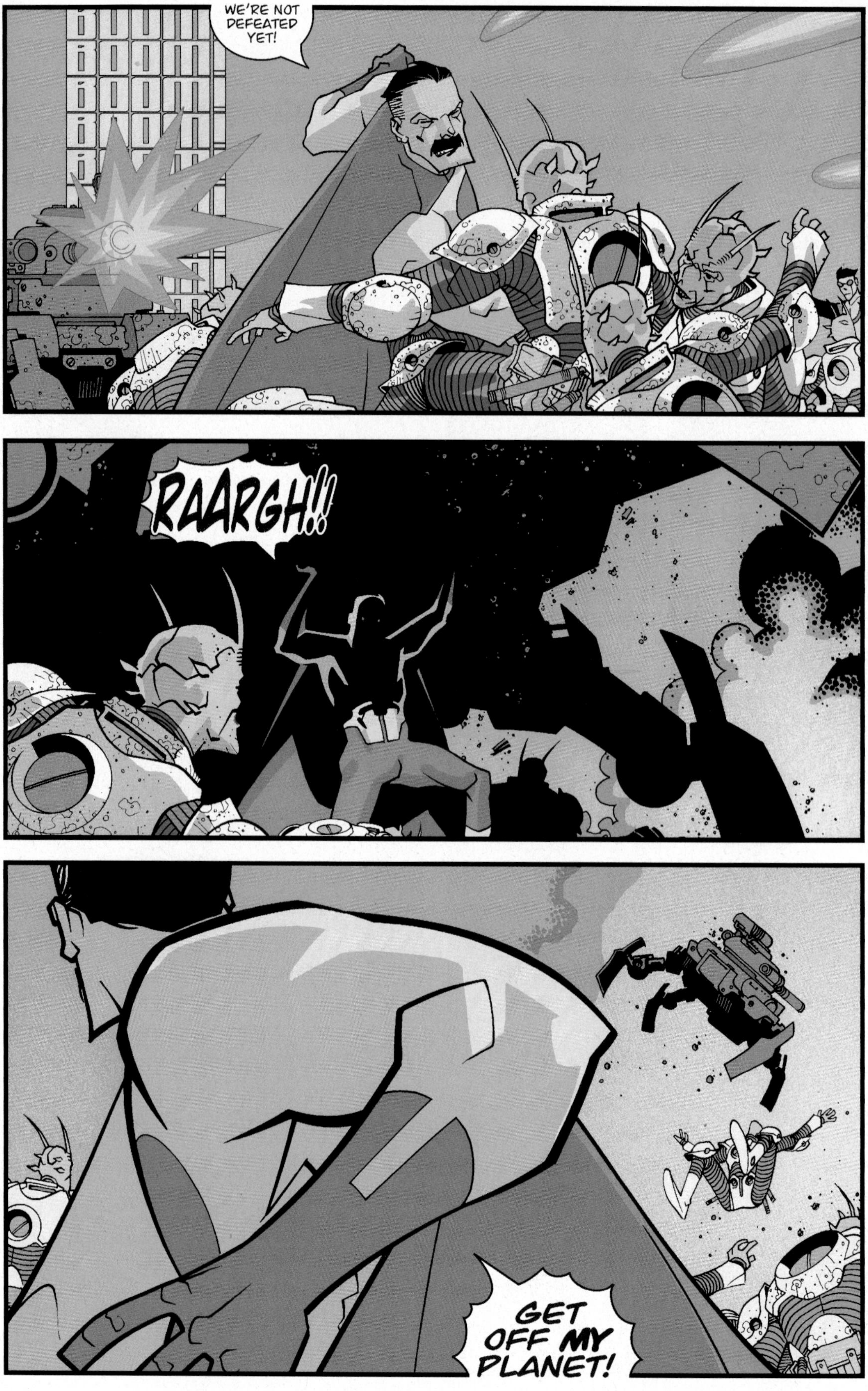
WE'RE NOT DEFEATED YET!
BOOM! BOOM! BOOM! BOOM!
RAARGH!!
GET OFF MY PLANET!

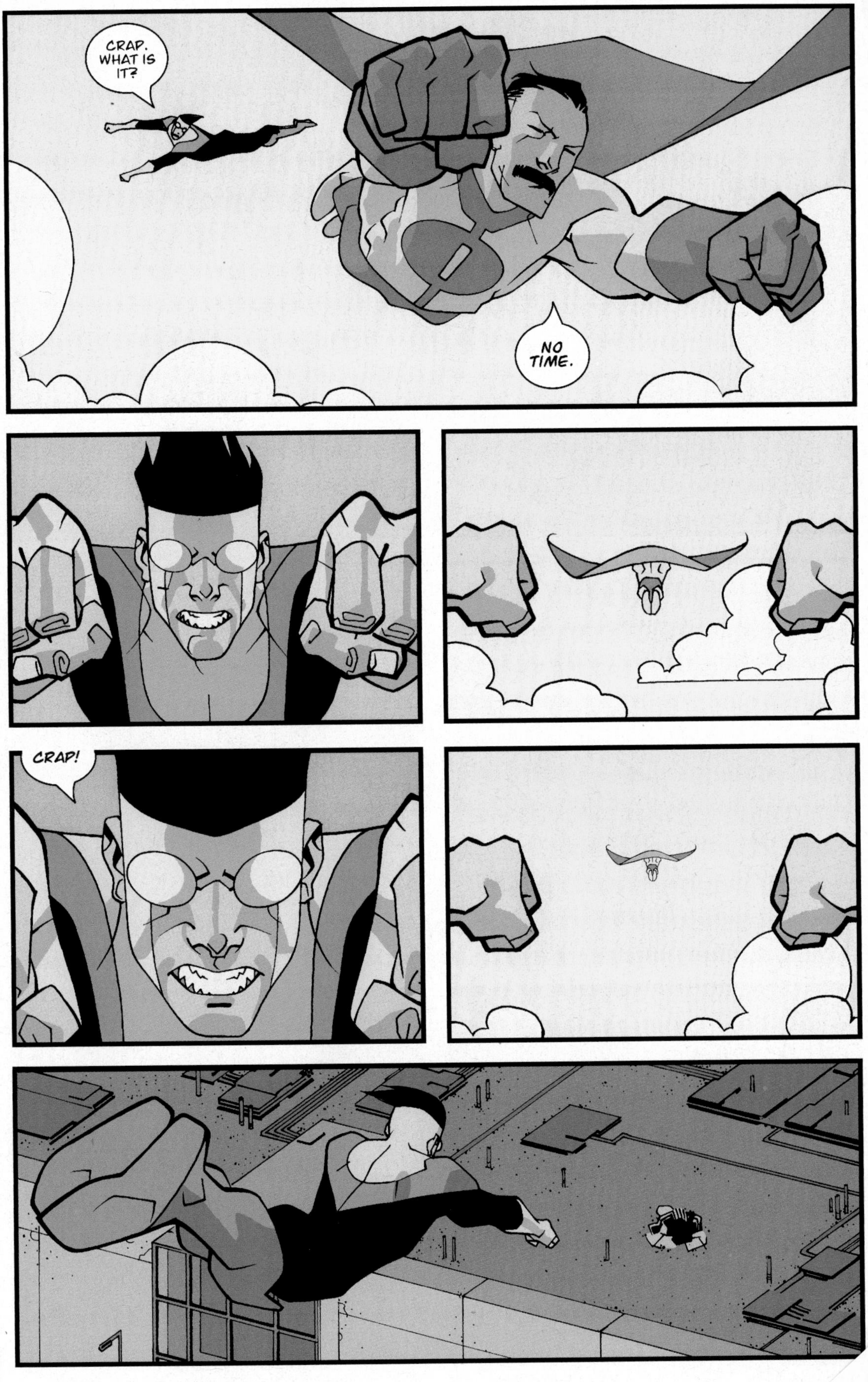
CRAP. WHAT IS IT?
NO TIME.
CRAP!

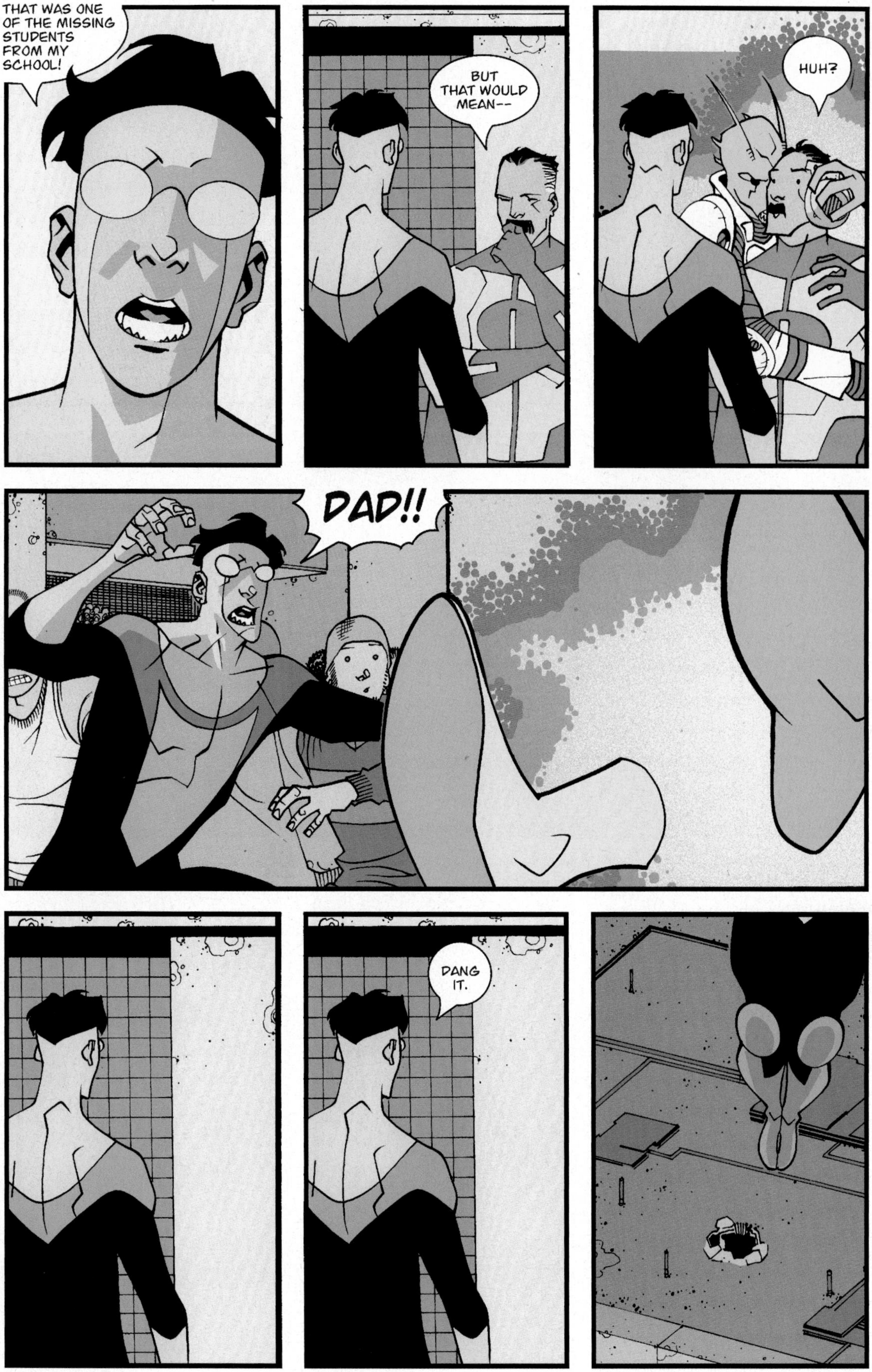
THAT WAS ONE OF THE MISSING STUDENTS FROM MY SCHOOL!
BUT THAT WOULD MEAN--
HUH?
DAD!!
DANG IT.

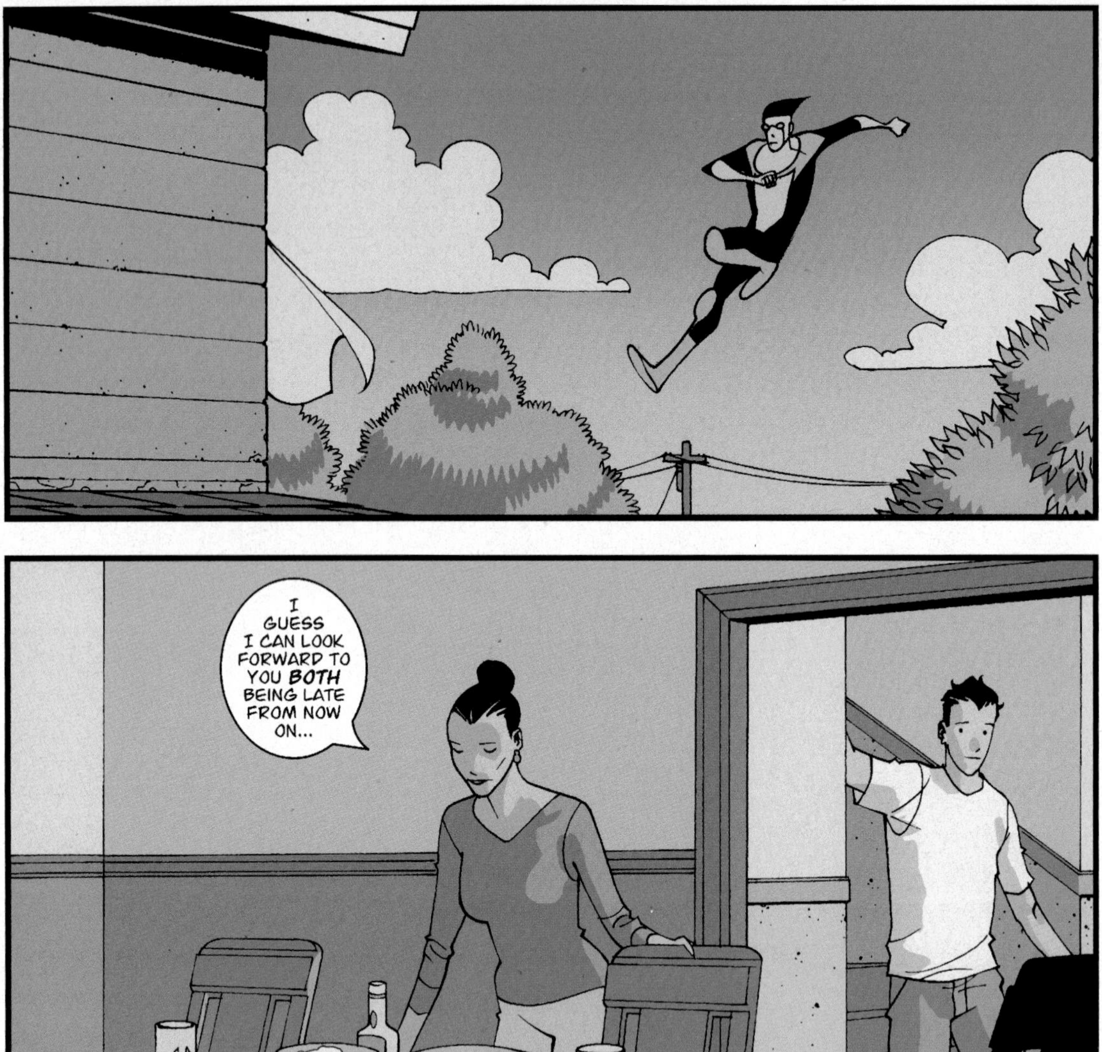
I GUESS I CAN LOOK FORWARD TO YOU **BOTH** BEING LATE FROM NOW ON...
ACTUALLY... DAD WAS SUCKED INTO A PORTAL ABOUT FIFTEEN MINUTES AGO, I DON'T THINK HE'LL BE HOME TONIGHT.
IT WAS SOME ALIENS WE FOUGHT EARLIER TODAY... I'M SURE HE'S FINE.
...
WELL, THAT'S MORE PORK CHOPS FOR US.

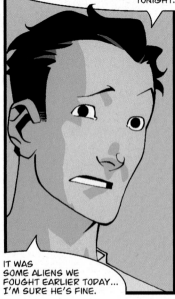

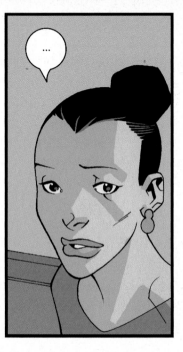

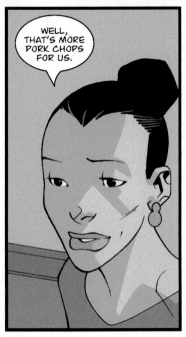

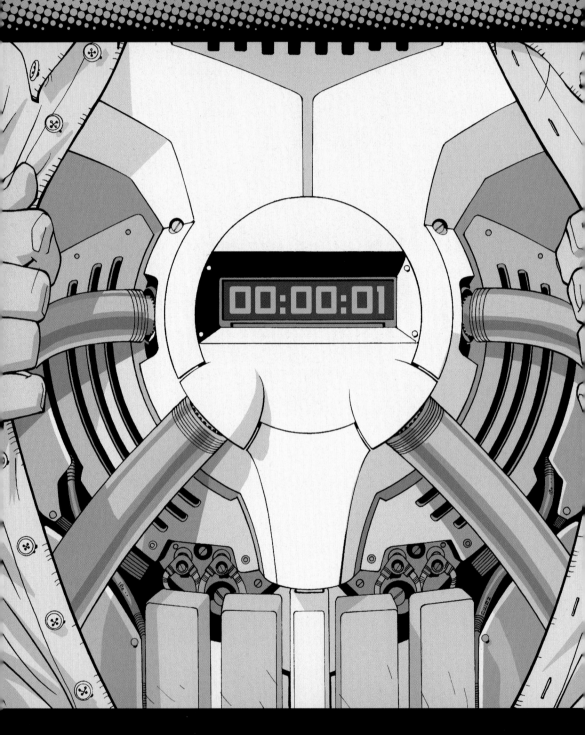

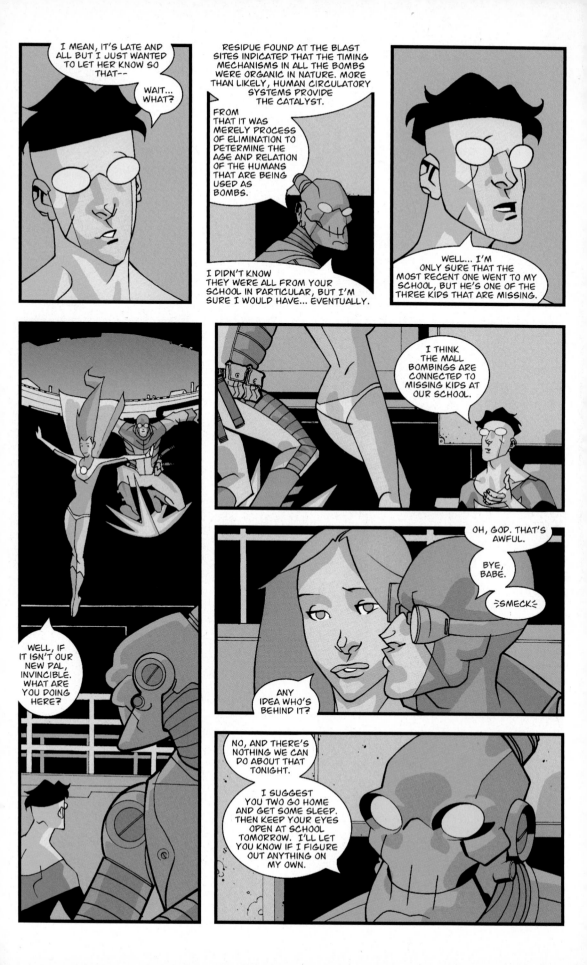

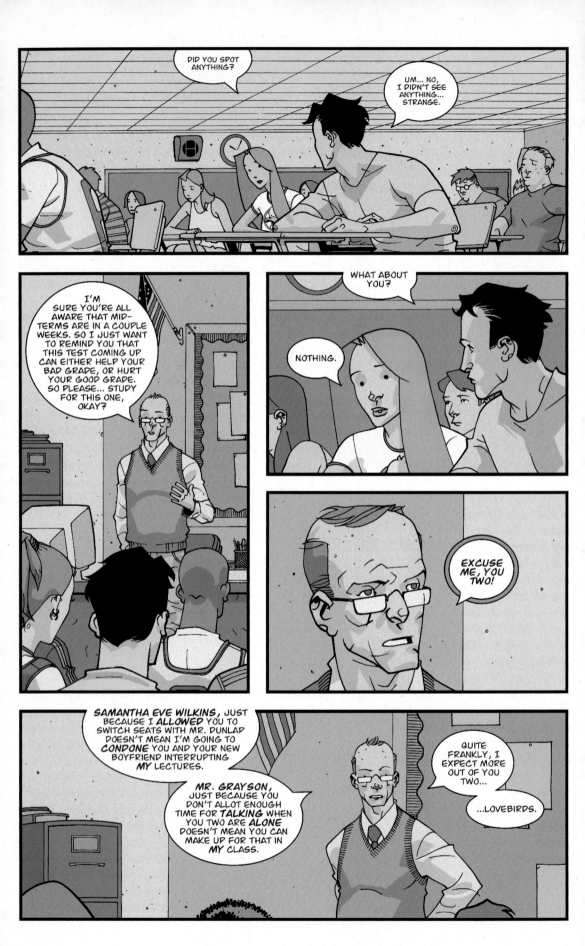

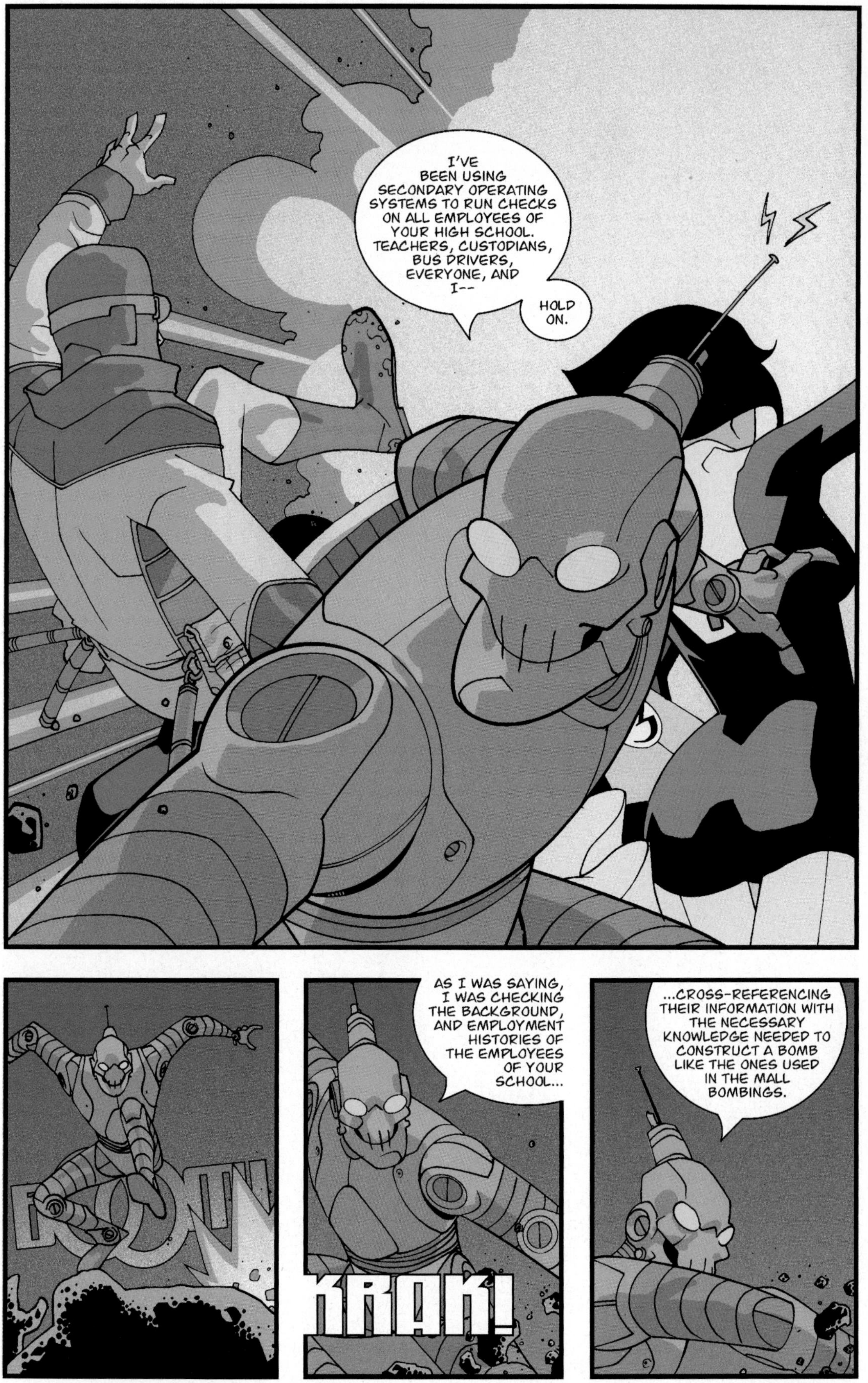
I'VE BEEN USING SECONDARY OPERATING SYSTEMS TO RUN CHECKS ON ALL EMPLOYEES OF YOUR HIGH SCHOOL. TEACHERS, CUSTODIANS, BUS DRIVERS, EVERYONE, AND I--
HOLD ON.
AS I WAS SAYING, I WAS CHECKING THE BACKGROUND, AND EMPLOYMENT HISTORIES OF THE EMPLOYEES OF YOUR SCHOOL...
KRAK!
...CROSS-REFERENCING THEIR INFORMATION WITH THE NECESSARY KNOWLEDGE NEEDED TO CONSTRUCT A BOMB LIKE THE ONES USED IN THE MALL BOMBINGS.

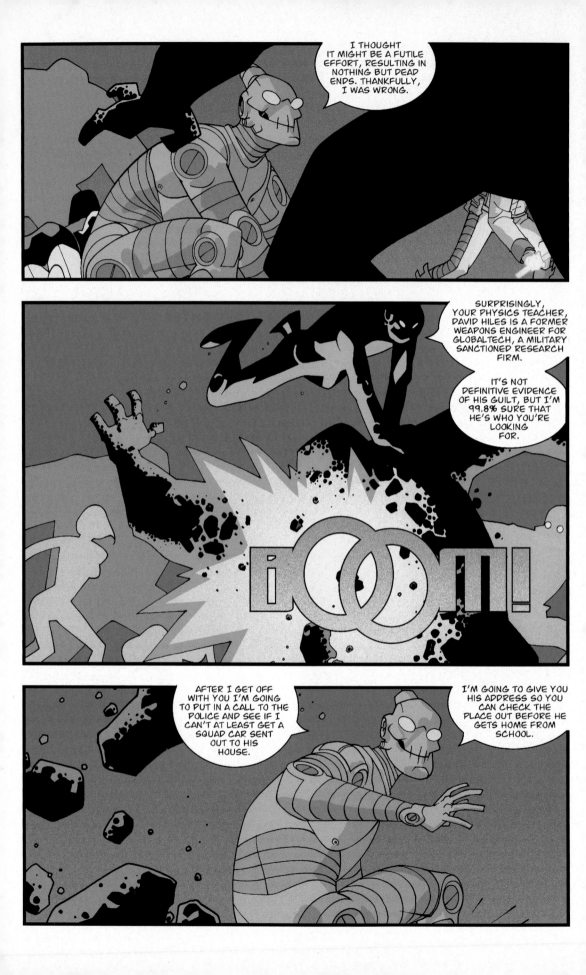

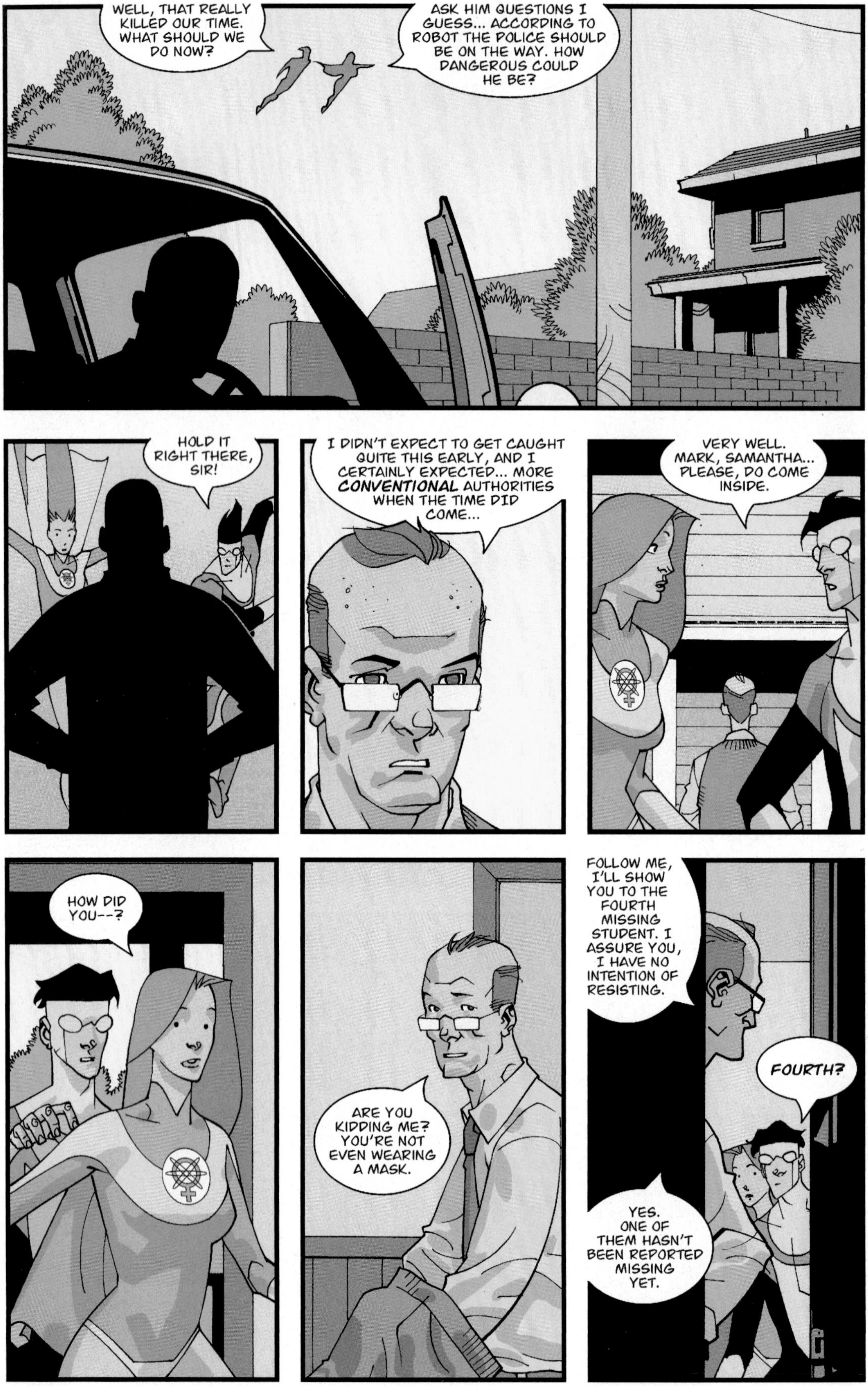
WELL, THAT REALLY KILLED OUR TIME. WHAT SHOULD WE DO NOW?
ASK HIM QUESTIONS I GUESS... ACCORDING TO ROBOT THE POLICE SHOULD BE ON THE WAY. HOW DANGEROUS COULD HE BE?
HOLD IT RIGHT THERE, SIR!
I DIDN'T EXPECT TO GET CAUGHT QUITE THIS EARLY, AND I CERTAINLY EXPECTED... MORE CONVENTIONAL AUTHORITIES WHEN THE TIME DID COME...
VERY WELL. MARK, SAMANTHA... PLEASE, DO COME INSIDE.
HOW DID YOU--?
ARE YOU KIDDING ME? YOU'RE NOT EVEN WEARING A MASK.
FOLLOW ME, I'LL SHOW YOU TO THE FOURTH MISSING STUDENT. I ASSURE YOU, I HAVE NO INTENTION OF RESISTING.
FOURTH?
YES. ONE OF THEM HASN'T BEEN REPORTED MISSING YET.

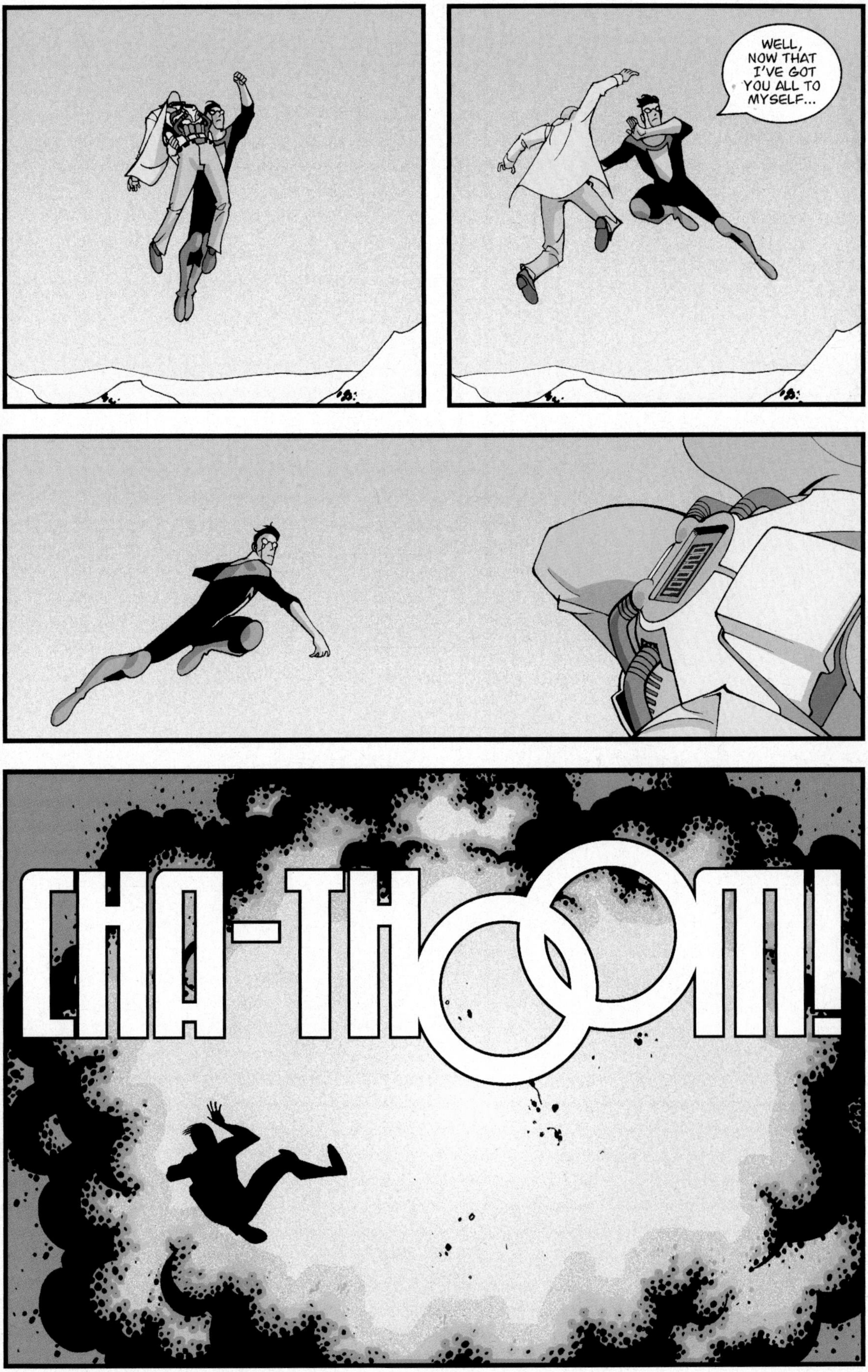
WELL, NOW THAT I'VE GOT YOU ALL TO MYSELF...
CHA-THOOM!

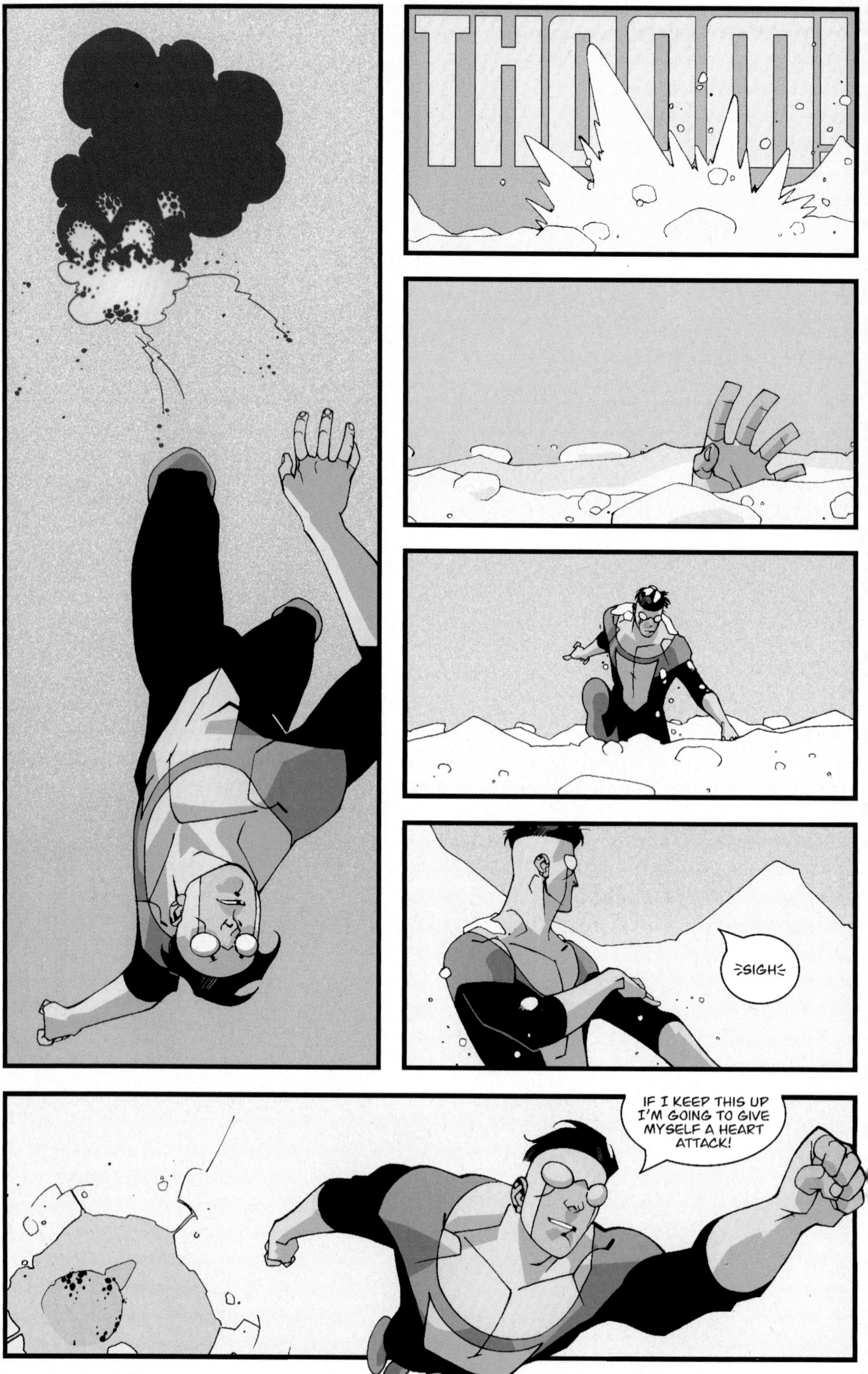
THOOOM!
SIGH
IF I KEEP THIS UP I'M GOING TO GIVE MYSELF A HEART ATTACK!

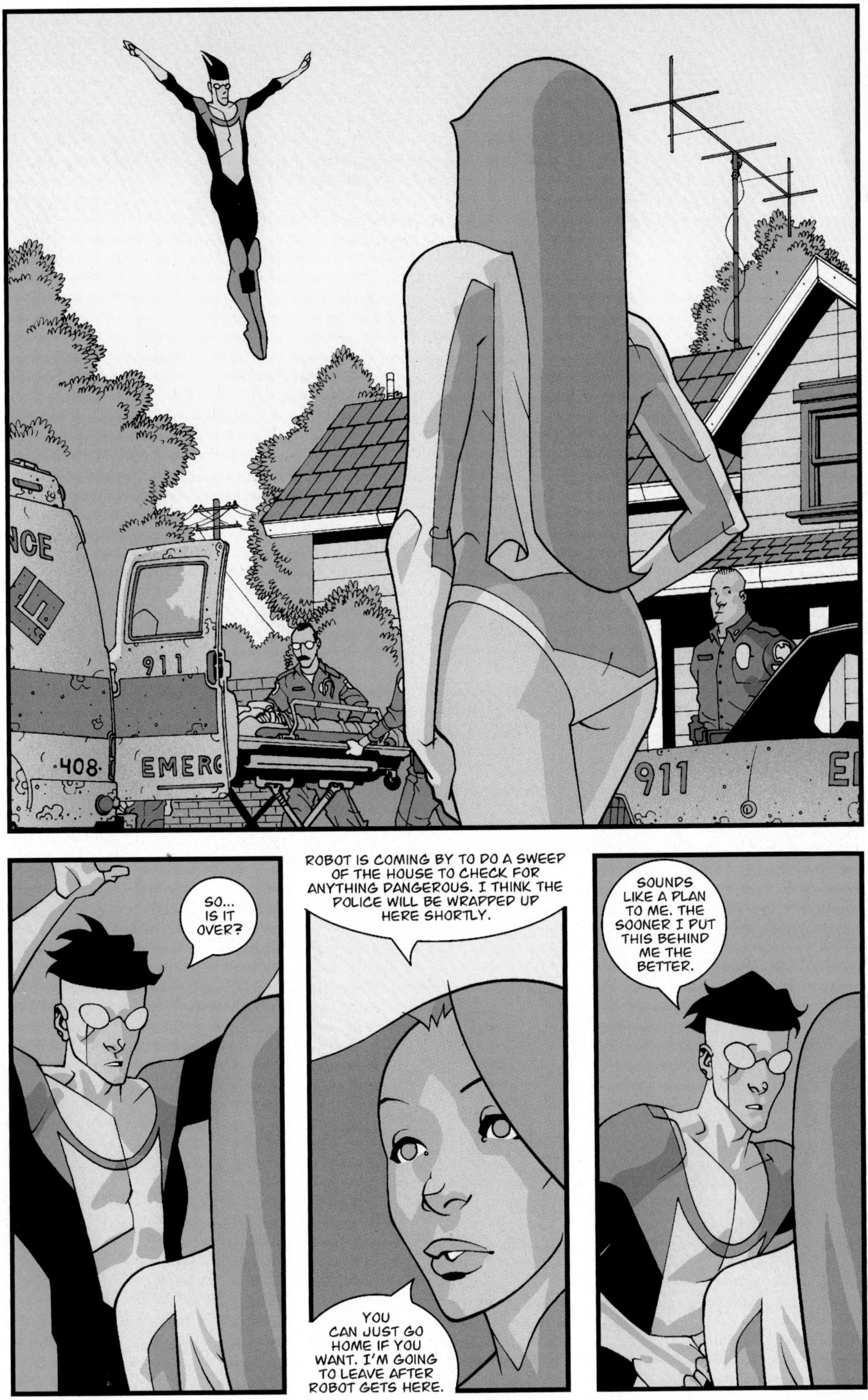
NCE
911
408
EMERG
911
SO... IS IT OVER?
ROBOT IS COMING BY TO DO A SWEEP OF THE HOUSE TO CHECK FOR ANYTHING DANGEROUS. I THINK THE POLICE WILL BE WRAPPED UP HERE SHORTLY.
YOU CAN JUST GO HOME IF YOU WANT. I'M GOING TO LEAVE AFTER ROBOT GETS HERE.
SOUNDS LIKE A PLAN TO ME. THE SOONER I PUT THIS BEHIND ME THE BETTER.

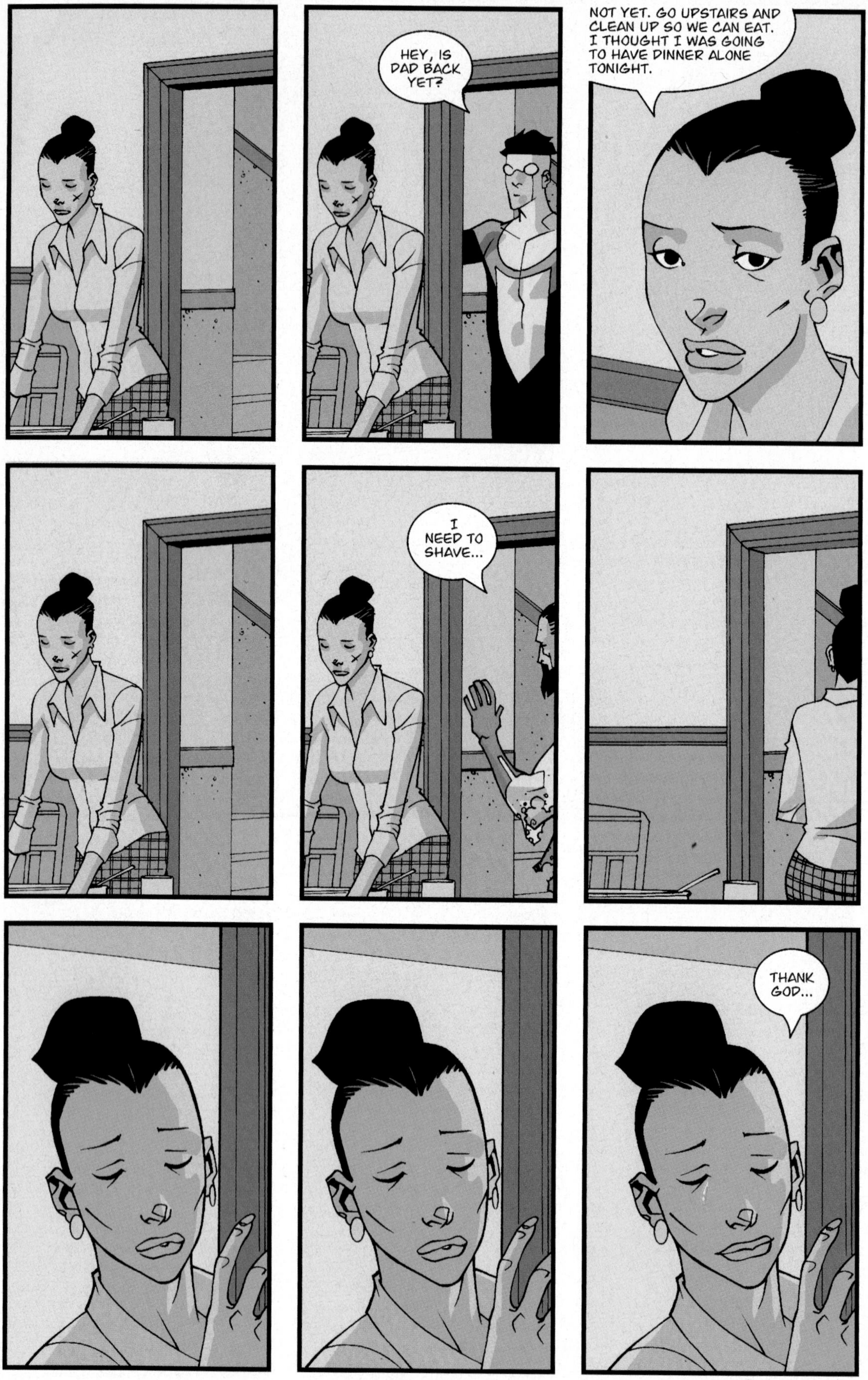
HEY, IS DAD BACK YET?
NOT YET. GO UPSTAIRS AND CLEAN UP SO WE CAN EAT. I THOUGHT I WAS GOING TO HAVE DINNER ALONE TONIGHT.
I NEED TO SHAVE...
THANK GOD...

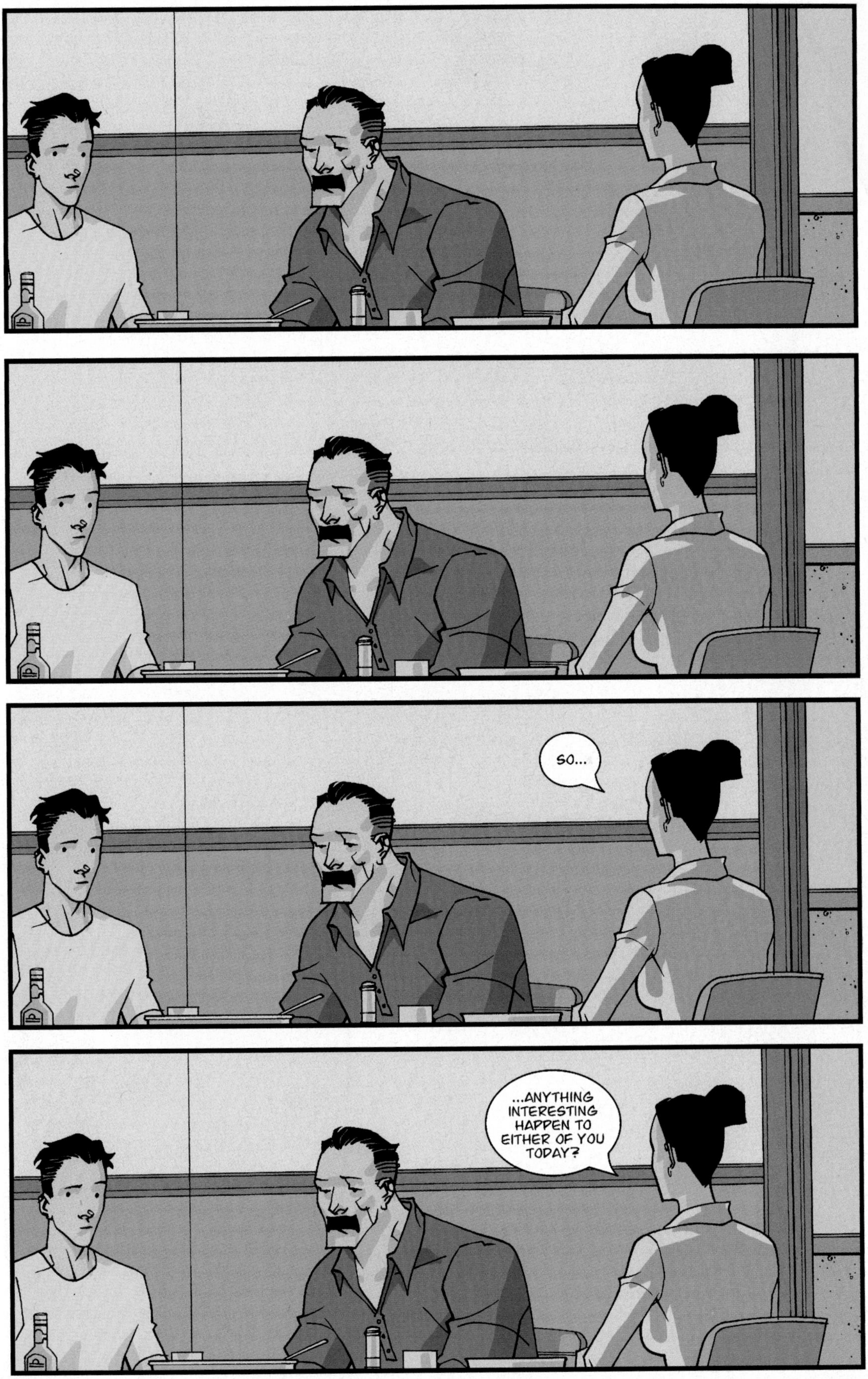
SO...
...ANYTHING INTERESTING HAPPEN TO EITHER OF YOU TODAY?

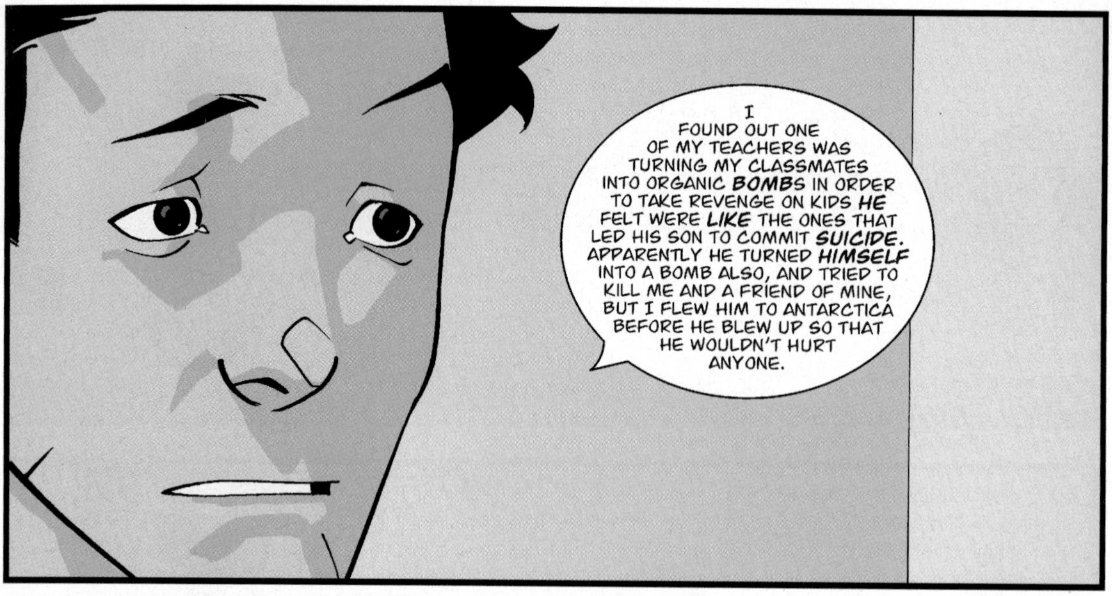

I FOUND OUT ONE OF MY TEACHERS WAS TURNING MY CLASSMATES INTO ORGANIC BOMBS IN ORDER TO TAKE REVENGE ON KIDS HE FELT WERE LIKE THE ONES THAT LED HIS SON TO COMMIT SUICIDE. APPARENTLY HE TURNED HIMSELF INTO A BOMB ALSO, AND TRIED TO KILL ME AND A FRIEND OF MINE, BUT I FLEW HIM TO ANTARCTICA BEFORE HE BLEW UP SO THAT HE WOULDN'T HURT ANYONE.

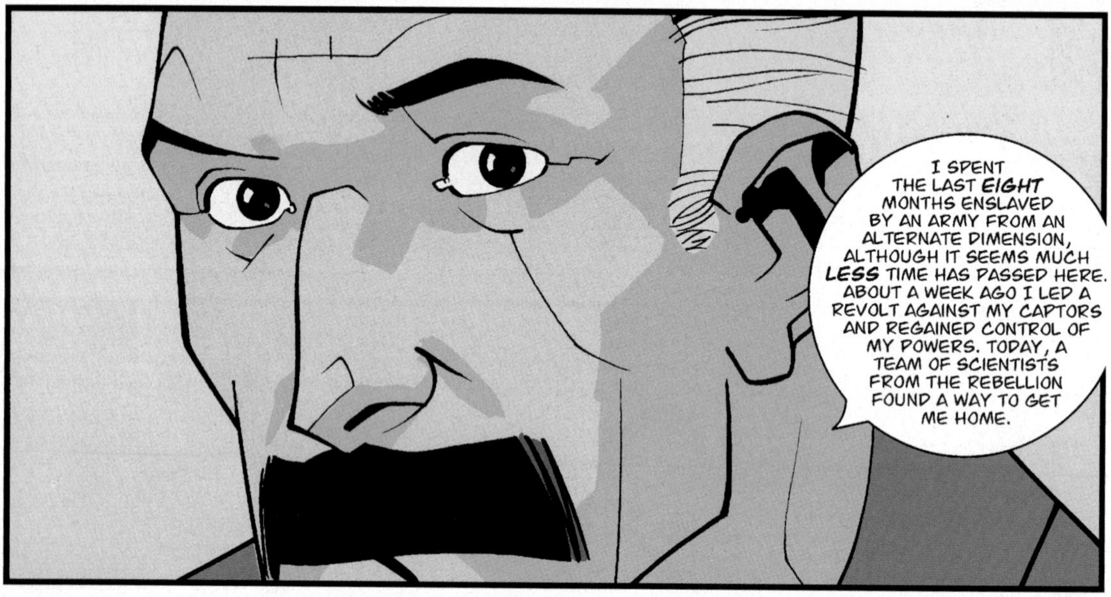

I SPENT THE LAST EIGHT MONTHS ENSLAVED BY AN ARMY FROM AN ALTERNATE DIMENSION, ALTHOUGH IT SEEMS MUCH LESS TIME HAS PASSED HERE. ABOUT A WEEK AGO I LED A REVOLT AGAINST MY CAPTORS AND REGAINED CONTROL OF MY POWERS. TODAY, A TEAM OF SCIENTISTS FROM THE REBELLION FOUND A WAY TO GET ME HOME.

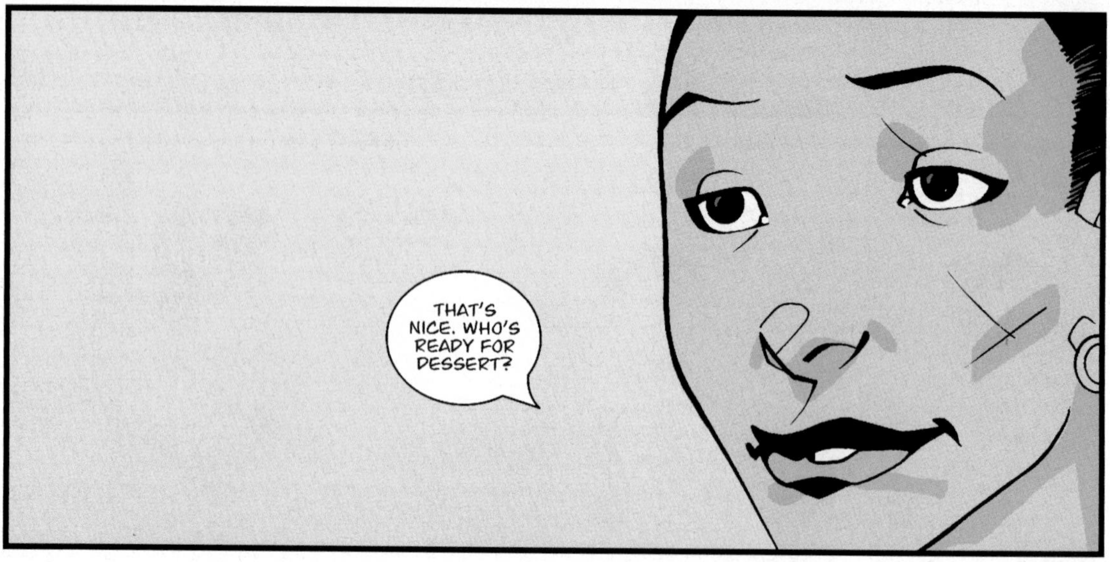

THAT'S NICE. WHO'S READY FOR DESSERT?

UNUSED COVERS

We went through a lot of versions of the first issue's cover. It all started out with a sketch I did of Mark flying up towards us with two bank robbers. Cory did the sketch below based on that, and it was pointed out that he'd look goofy if he smiled, and that he was flying from right to left. Since we read from left to right things flow better in comics if they MOVE in that direction too. Both of these problems were my fault. So Cory took over and came up with the second sketch you see... doesn't Mark look serious? The cover was finished up and sent to Val Staples to color, this was before Bill Crabtree came on board. Val did a hell of a job and I've always loved the way his stuff looks on Cory's work but there was a problem... the colors were WRONG!! And Jim Valentino said the overly blue background made him want to go to sleep... and this is the LAST thing we want to do to potential readers.

Val was swamped at this time, trying to launch that nifty *Masters of the Universe* comic so with his approval, Cory and I got our good pal Tony Moore to alter Val's version, changing the background and making the white on the costume yellow.

Later Cory and I decided that we weren't too keen on Mark's serious facial expression, so Cory altered the line art to make him smile just a little... and I requested some money be thrown in the air to play up the bank robbing angle. Around this time, young Bill Crabtree had come aboard. So he colored the version seen on the opposite page.

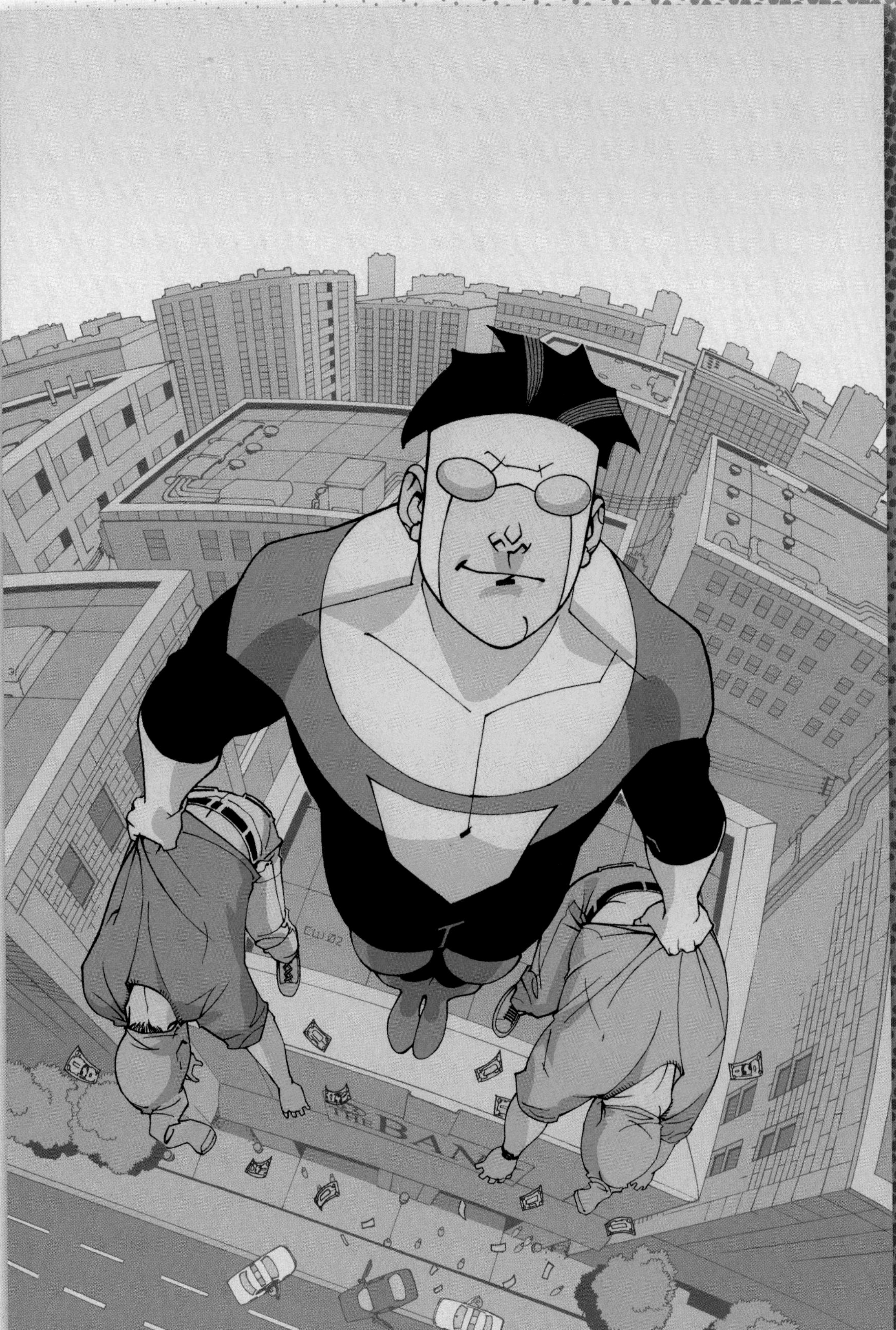

After all the initial promotion was out of the way... it was brought to our attention by Image that the original cover wasn't as strong as it could be and in their opinion would hurt our sales. That's not the smartest thing to do, so Cory immediately started burning the midnight oil trying to come up with something new. My pal Erik Larsen even threw his hat into the ring with the sketch below, and we were going to use it until Jim Valentino remembered a promo image Cory had done and thought it would make the perfect cover. Cory then took that image and came up with a new background for it. It was decided that reading the paper and washing dishes weren't very exciting, Jim suggested expanding the cracked wall panel that's behind Mark into the entire background... and thus, a cover was born.

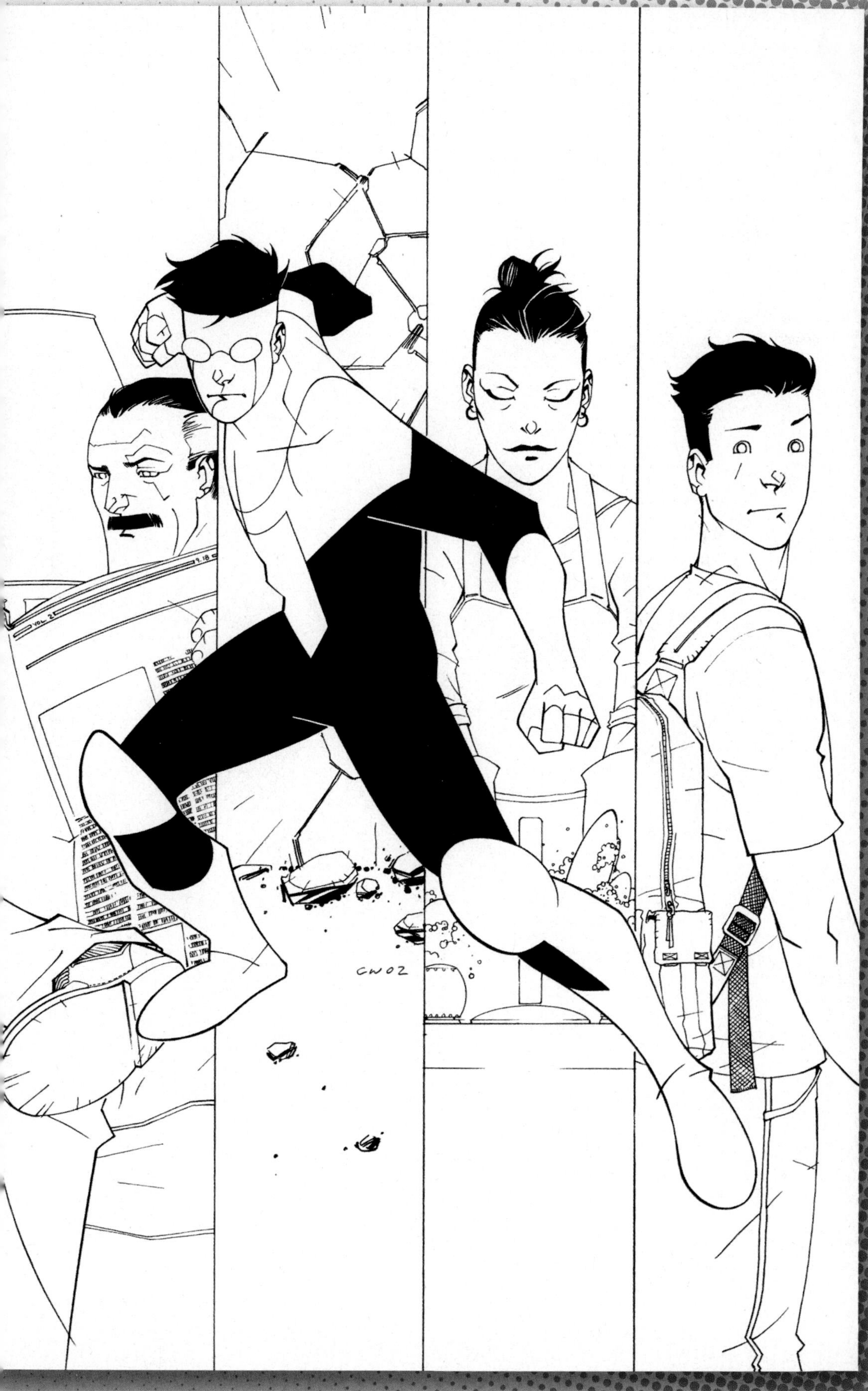

PROMOTIONAL ART

Cory and I really wanted to have a Previews ad that was more than just a cover, so we did the page that you see on the opposite page, and all the illos seen below. Then Diamond stopped allowing Image enough space to do two-page solicitations for the first issues, and we didn't use any of it. Here's the image that became the cover for issue one, and Atom Eve's original costume. Actually most of the Teen Team is different in that picture below.

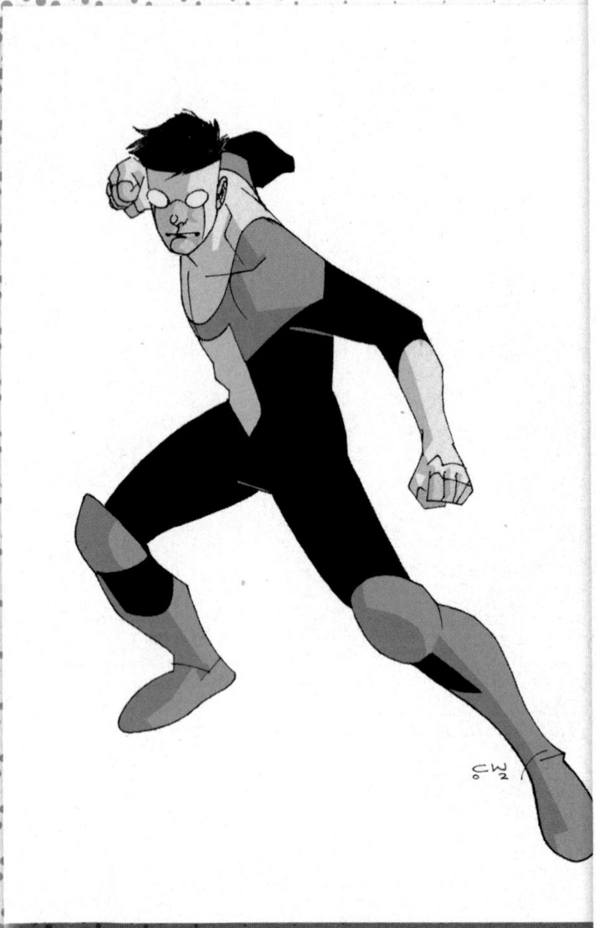

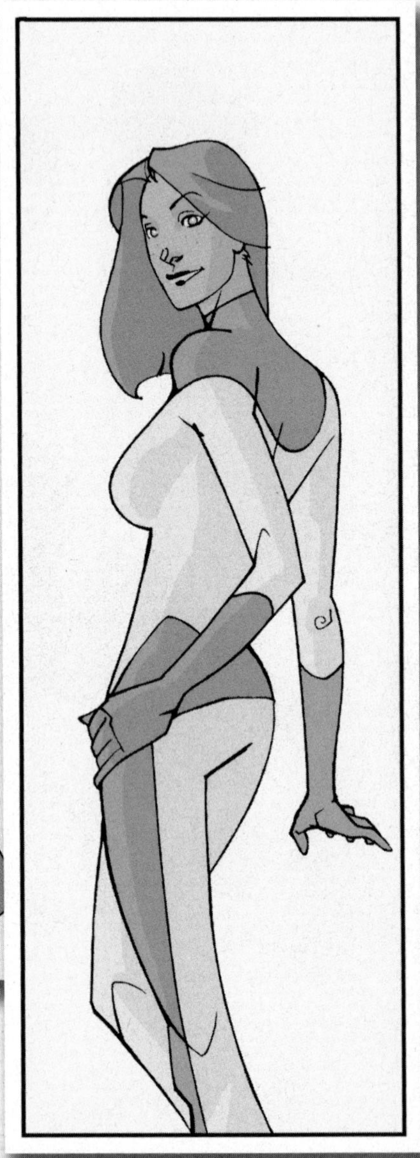

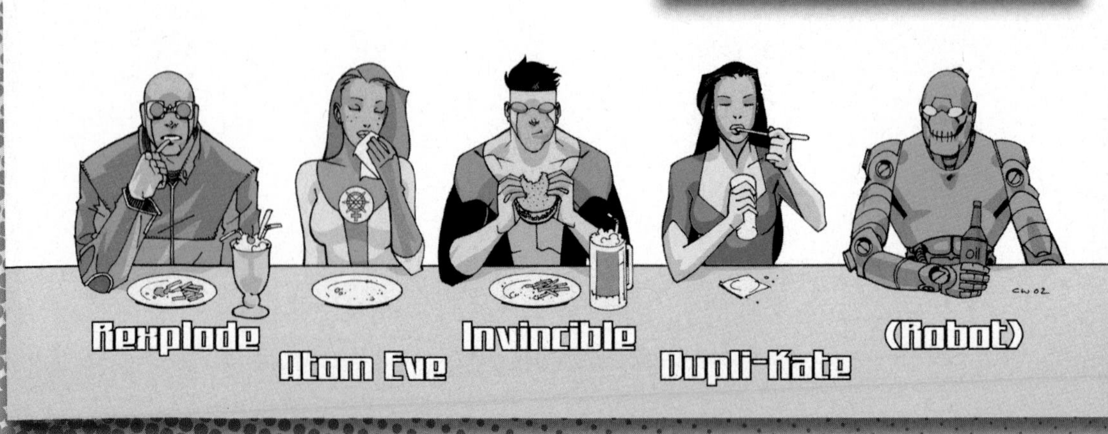
Rexplode
Atom Eve
Invincible
Dupli-Kate
(Robot)

It's a little known fact that Invincible was originally going to be called 'Bulletproof.' The name was changed because Image was publishing *Bulletproof Monk* and they thought it would conflict. Thank god for small miracles, huh? The first image below was going to be the cover of our proposal. This was the original Bulletproof costume. With the name changed, though... Cory and I wanted to somehow work in the letter 'I' to try and make the costume more iconic. Cory came up with the design that's used now and the proposal cover was changed at the last minute. And Yes, he was originally orange instead of blue, but the Bulletproof costume was yellow and blue... I guess we had it right the first time.

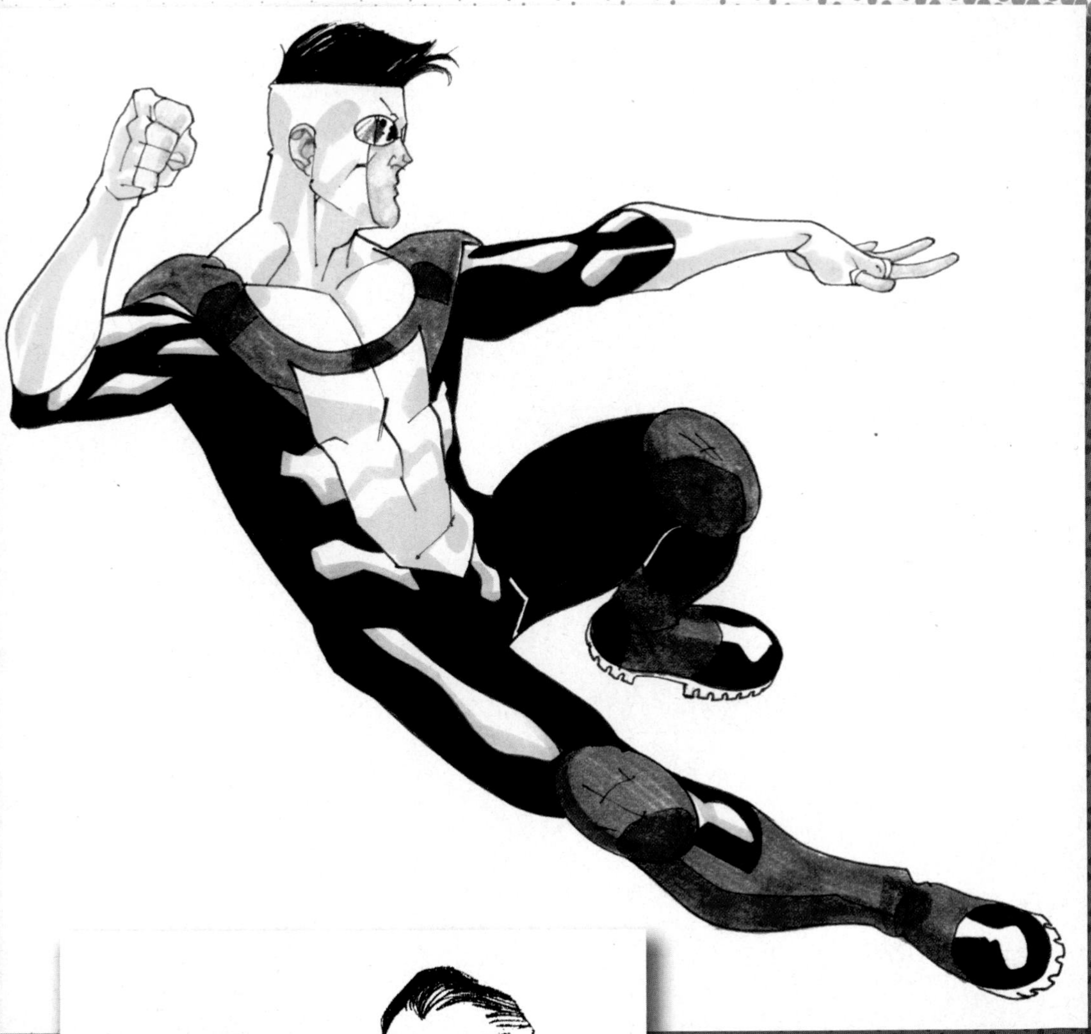

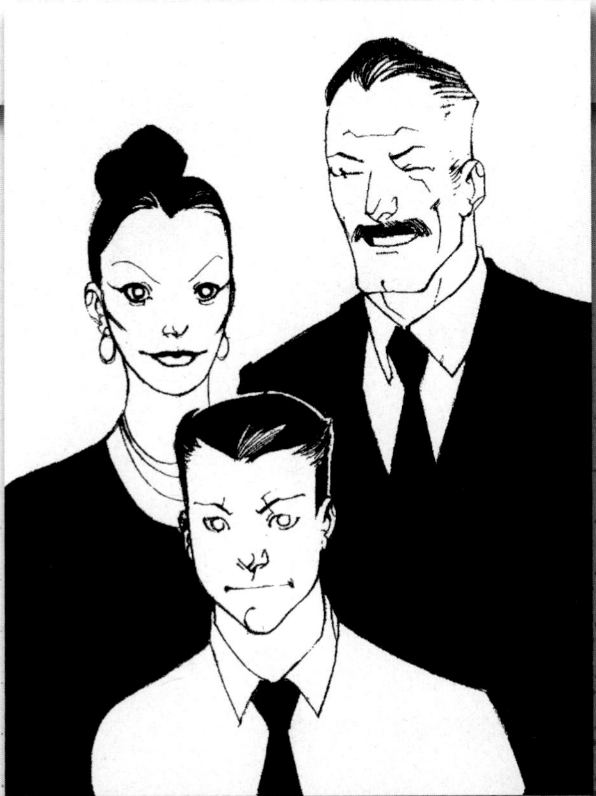

I wanted to see what the costume would look like with gray instead of orange... it wasn't one of my better ideas. There's a funny story about this family portrait. In issue two of the Saint Michael mini-series I did with Terry Stevens, there's a panel where there's a Science Dog, SuperPatriot and Superman poster on the wall, along with a family portrait hanging in the hallway that looks just like this picture. Aside from Superman these are all books Cory and I have worked on together. The page was also drawn a full year before we knew anything about doing SuperPatriot or Invincible. Let's see if we somehow end up on Superman next...

SKETCHES

Below is the first ever drawing on Bulletproof/Invincible, as well as a couple other drawings from when he was called Bulletproof. Originally... Mark's powers were going to be solar power-based, and the disks were going to be designed by Robot to store solar energy in case of an emergency. Then he was going to have an invisible aura around him that altered the density of stuff to make him able to fly... and super strong... and stuff... but then I found out that's what Jay Faerber and Jamal Igle's guy, Venture did. Now... well... where's the fun if it's explained.

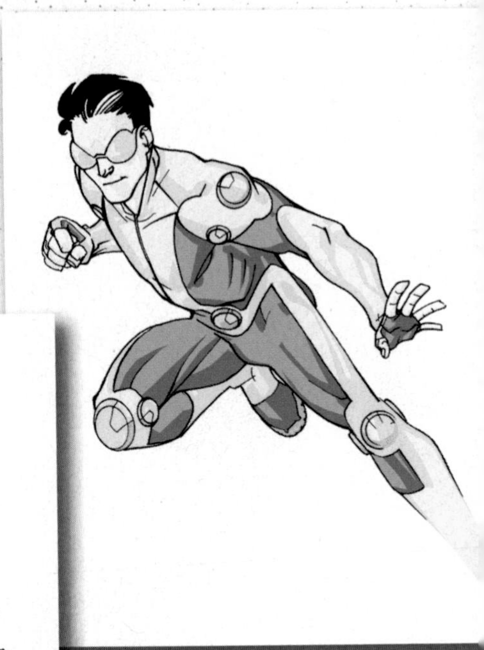

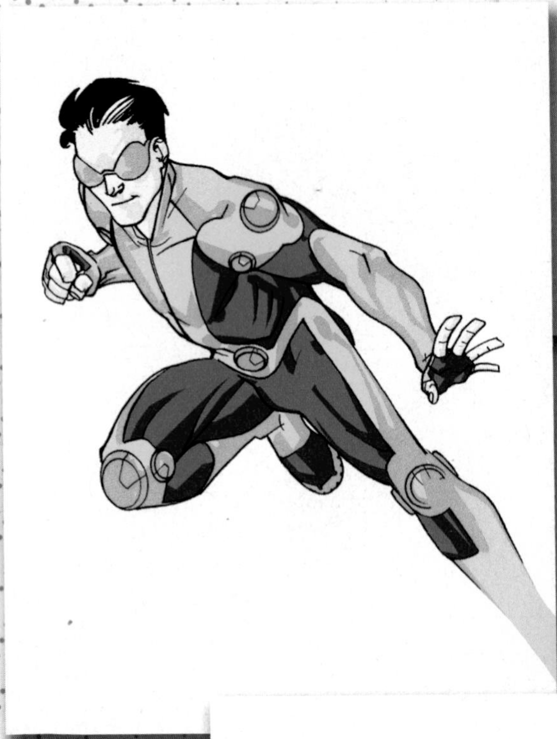

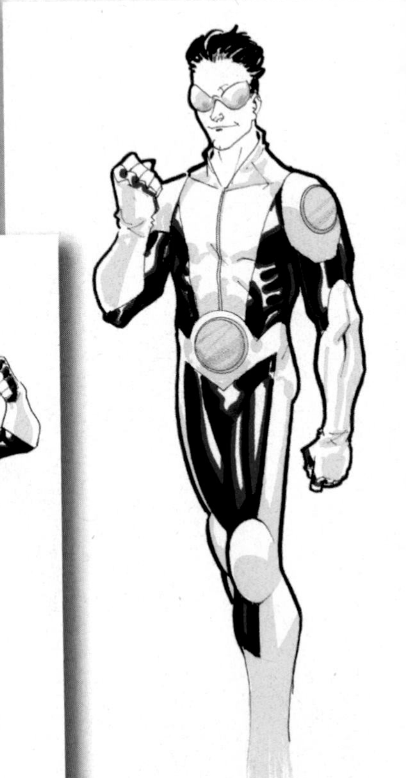

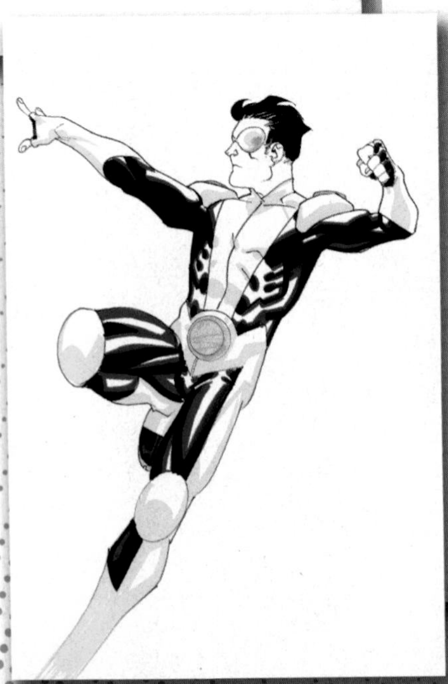

Below are some sketches by me, I'm sure you'll have no trouble picking them out. One was an attempt at putting an 'I' on the Bulletproof costume before Cory came up with the new design that we went with. Another little known fact is that when Invincible was called Bulletproof, Omni-Man was called Supra-Man. Image made us change it fearing that DC might not enjoy us using a name that when pronounced out loud is almost impossible to distinguish from their beloved trademark character. I really liked the undies that Supra-Man wore. When Cory remembered that Nolan came to earth in the '80s and wouldn't really have a classic looking costume, we scrapped this look and went with a more modern one.

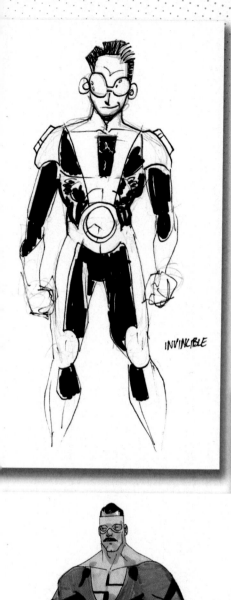

INVINCIBLE

SUPRAMAN

SUPRA-MAN
MAN OF STUFF

Here are some early designs for the Teen Team, and the first drawing of the more 'modern' costume for Supra-Man/Omni-Man. Robot was all Cory's idea... I really just came up with the know-it-all personality to go with the design. Cory also came up with the BRILLIANT name Atom Eve... but Rex Splode and Dupli-Kate are all me. Some people think the Teen Team's names are a little funky... I prefer to think of them as awesome.

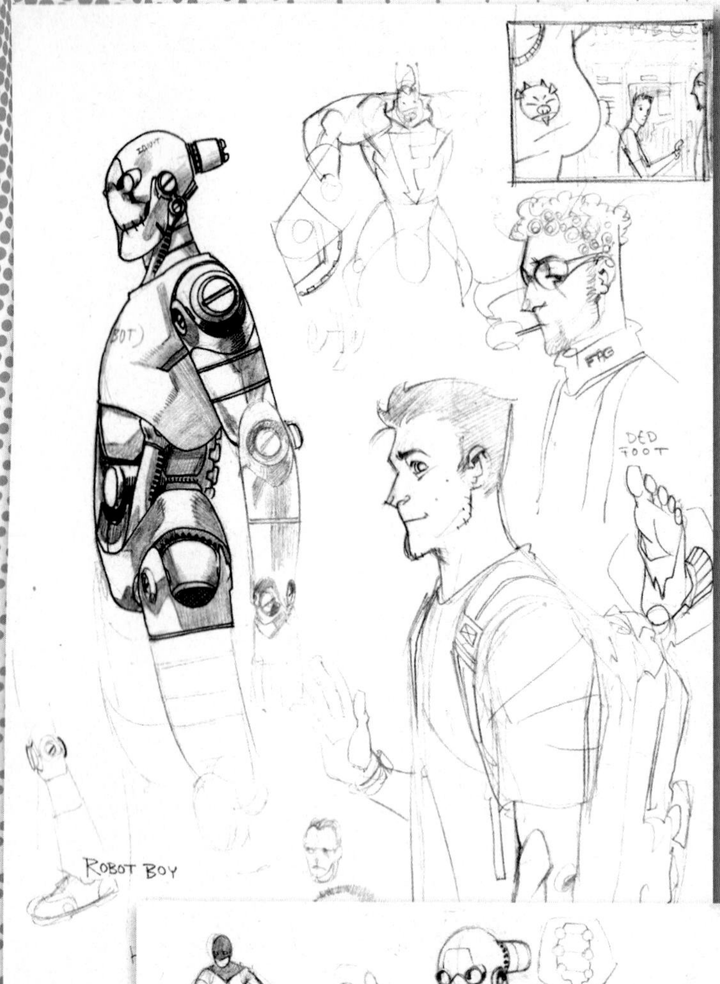
ROBOT BOY

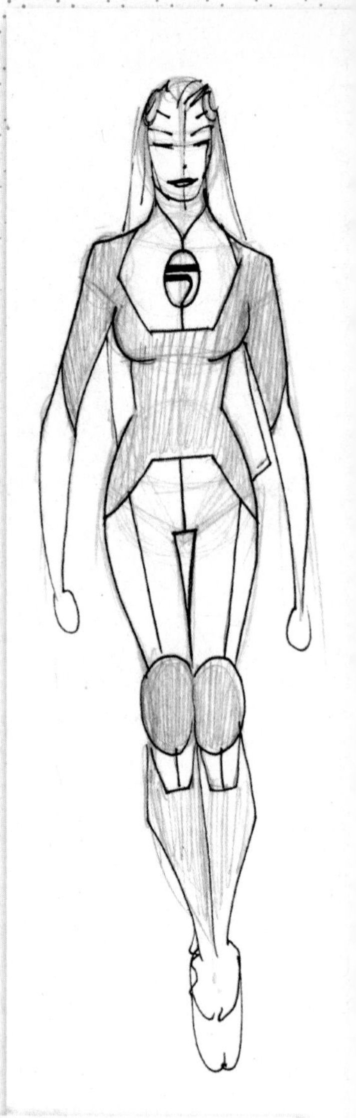

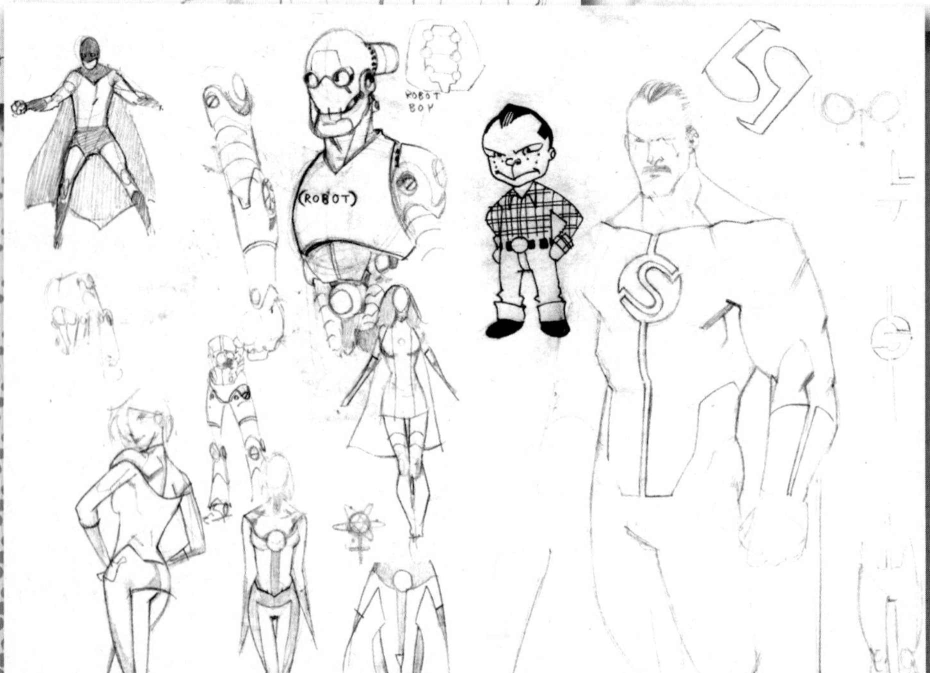
(ROBOT)
ROBOT BOY
ATOM EVE

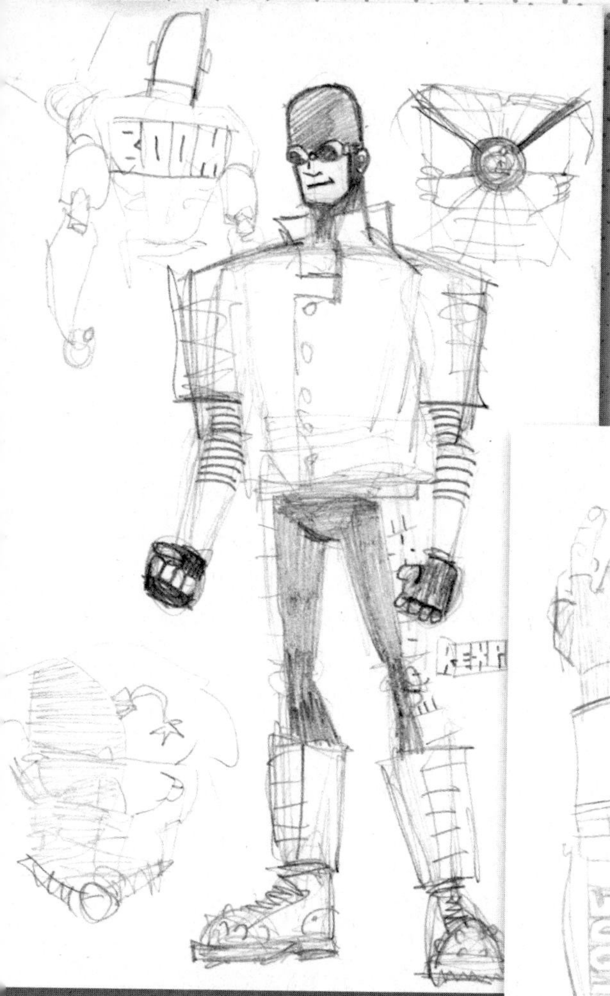
REXP

Here's my original design for Rex Splode and Cory's revision. Originally, his name was supposed to be printed on the side of his leg. I thought it might be a little too hard to draw all the time and to be honest... it might have been a bit to '90s. I think it looks better without it. Also on this page... Invincible with a knife in his shoulder. 'Invincible' indeed.

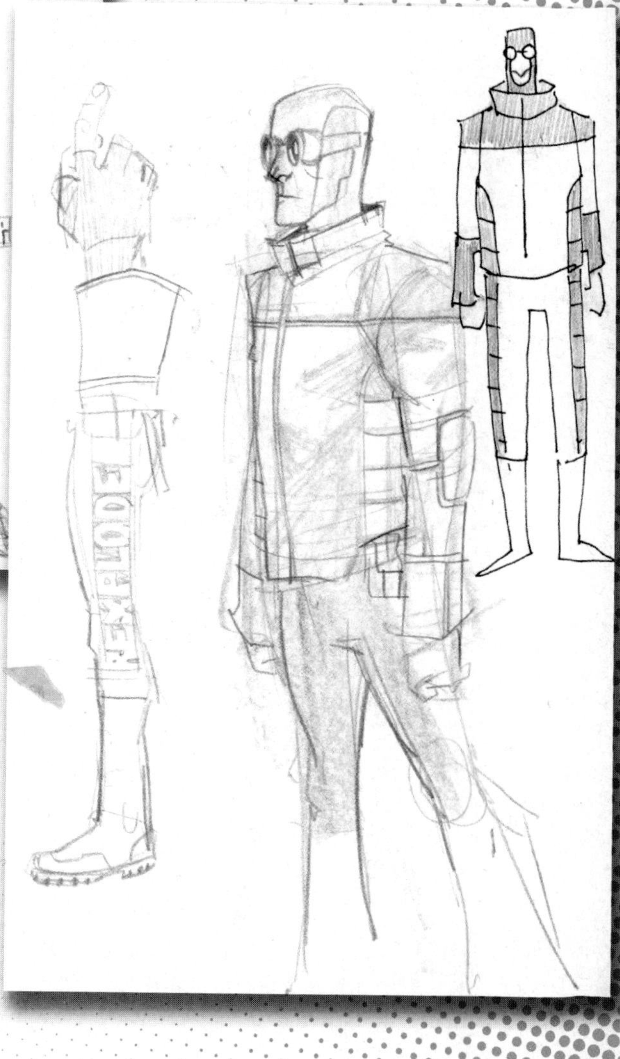

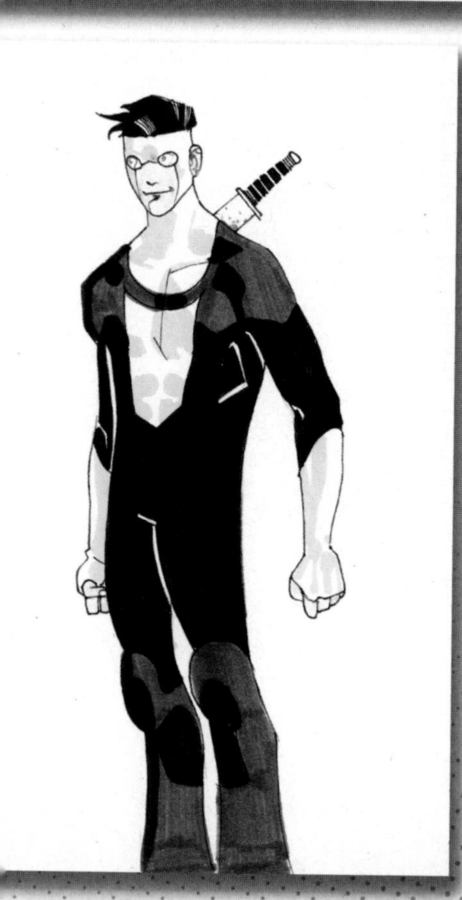

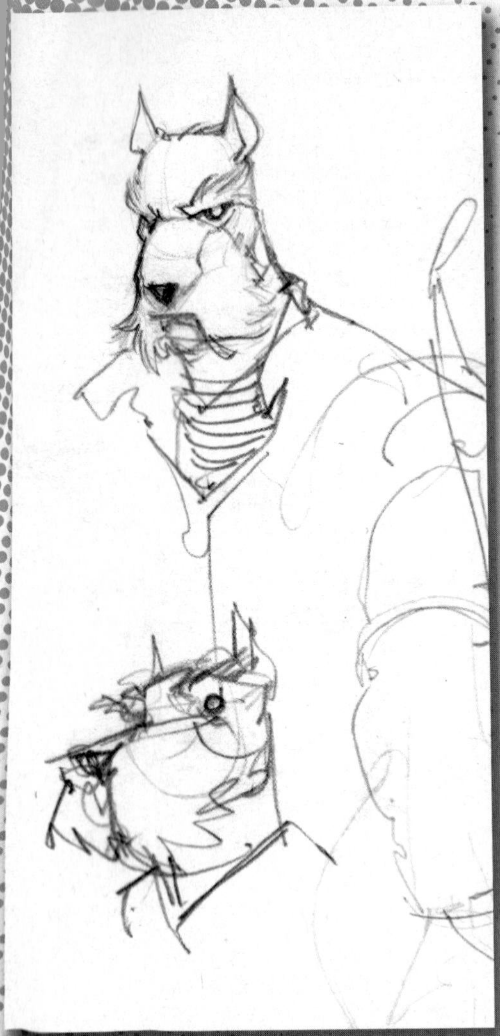

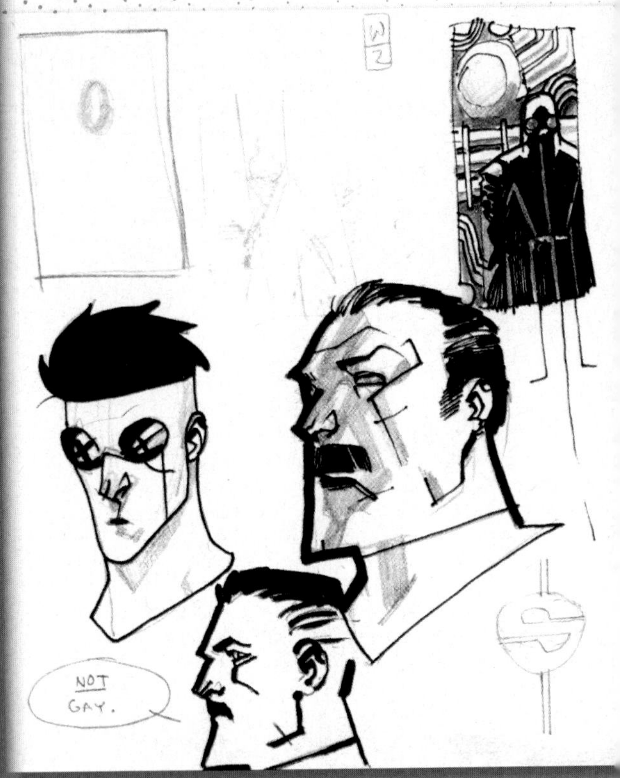
NOT GAY.

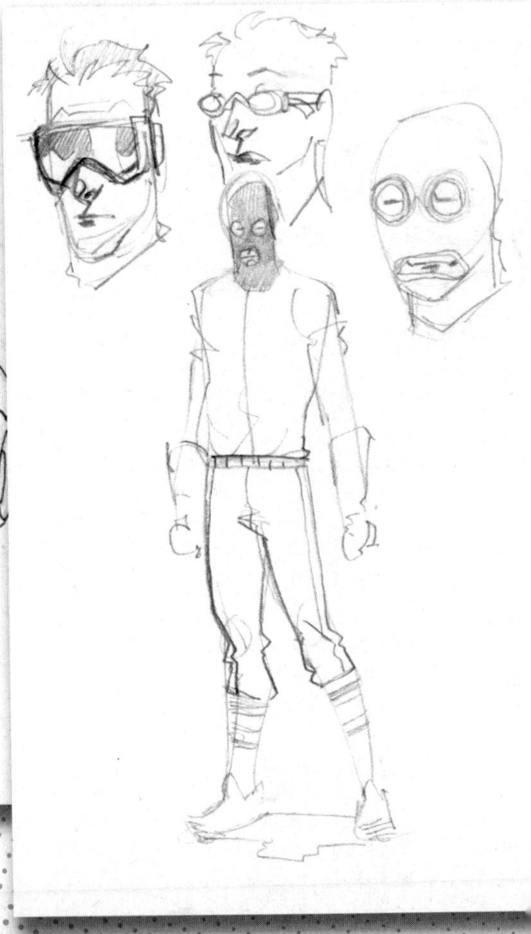

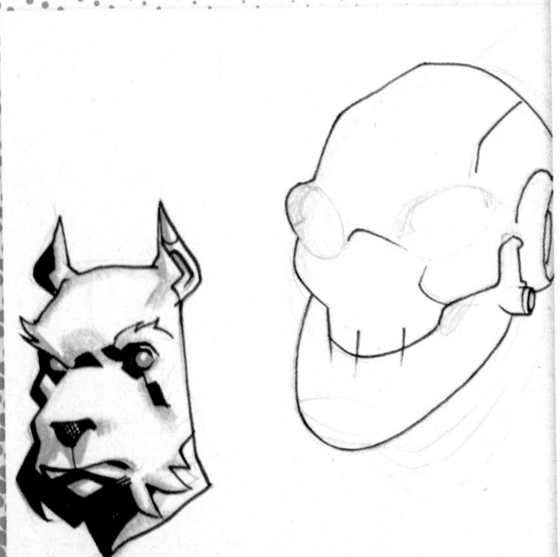

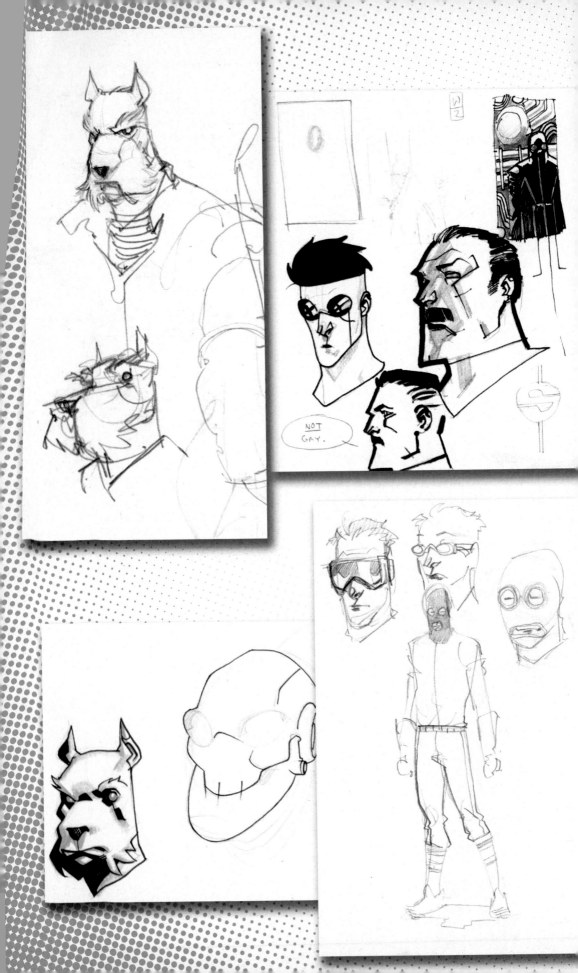

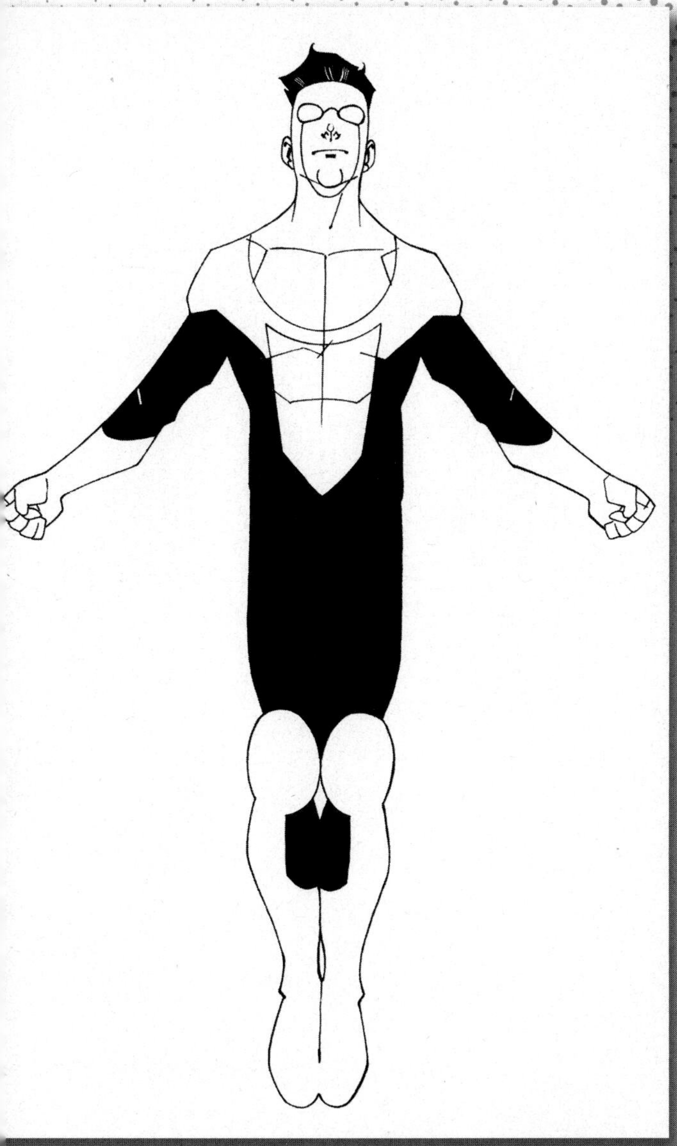

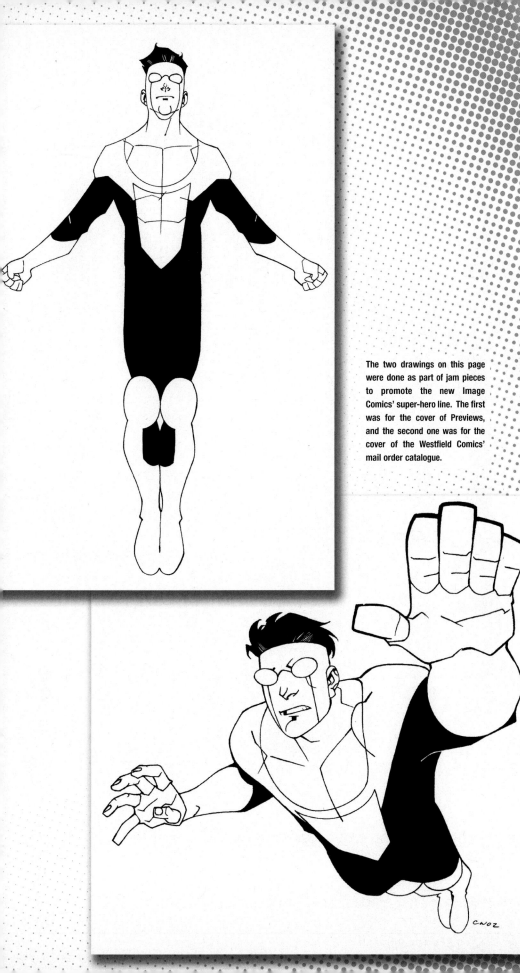

The two drawings on this page were done as part of jam pieces to promote the new Image Comics' super-hero line. The first was for the cover of Previews, and the second one was for the cover of the Westfield Comics' mail order catalogue.

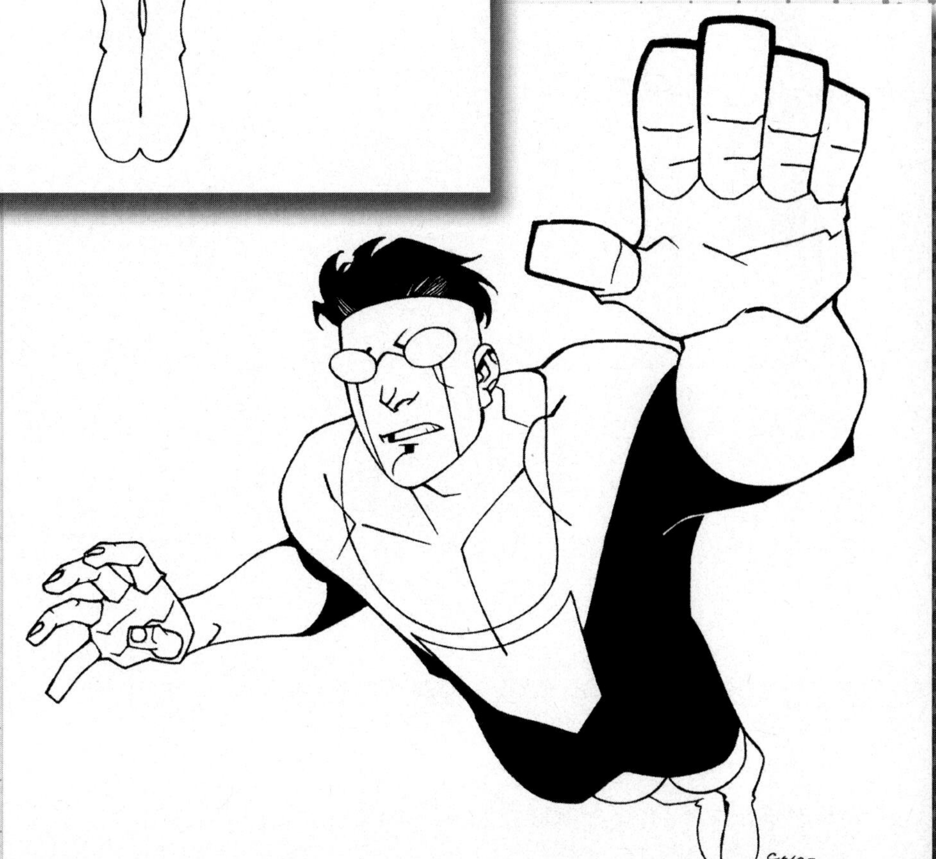
CWOZ

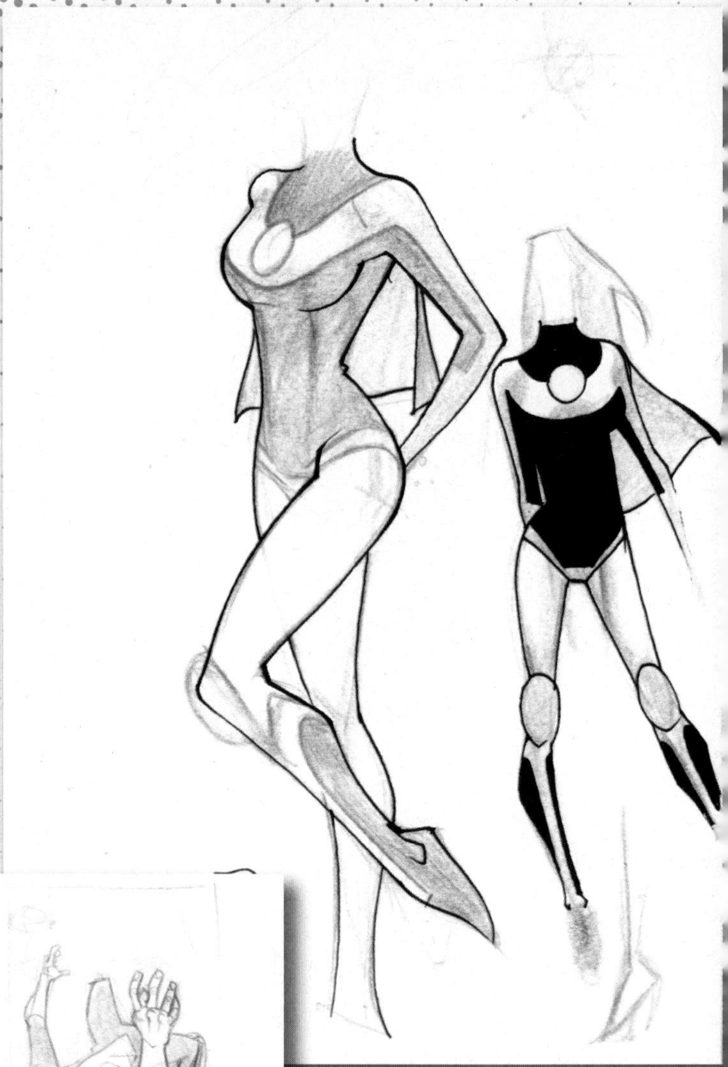

When it came time to work on Invincible issue two, featuring the first appearance of the Teen Team, Cory decided to make Eve's costume a bit sexier. I think it was a good move, it's a much better costume. It would be negligent of me if I didn't mention that the itty-bitty cape was my idea.

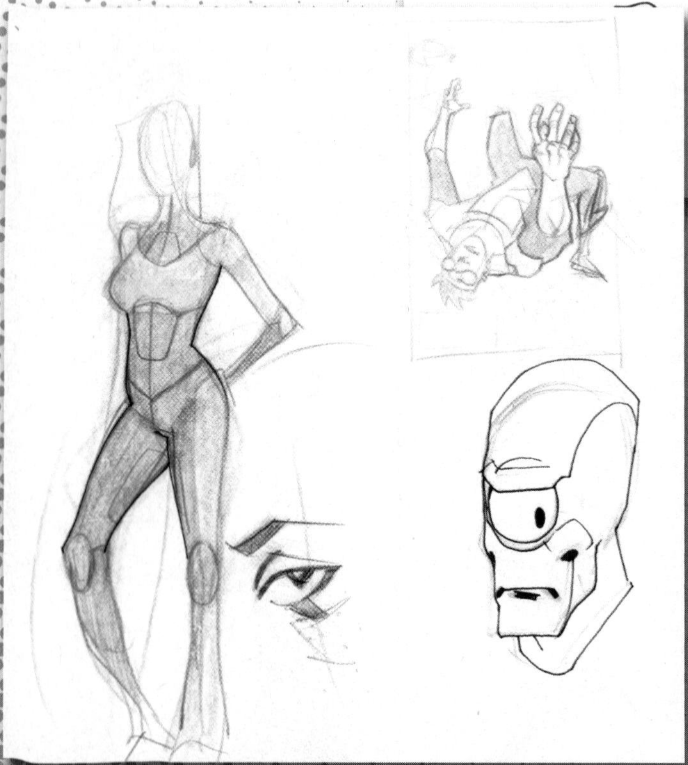

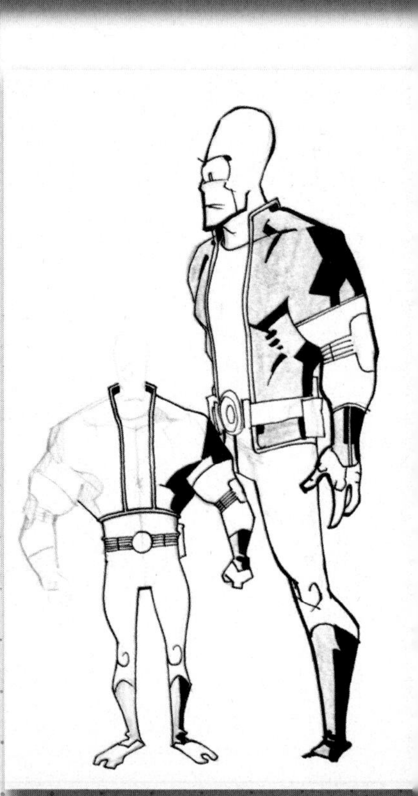

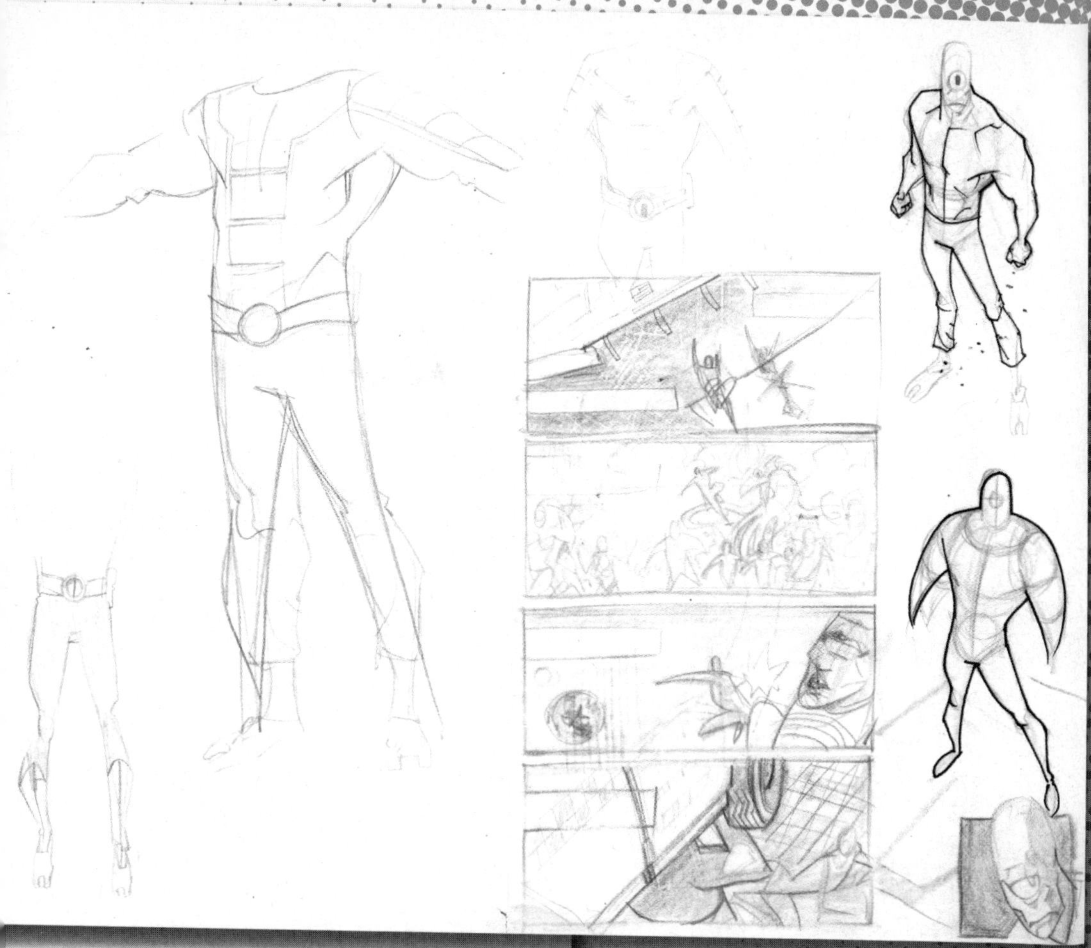

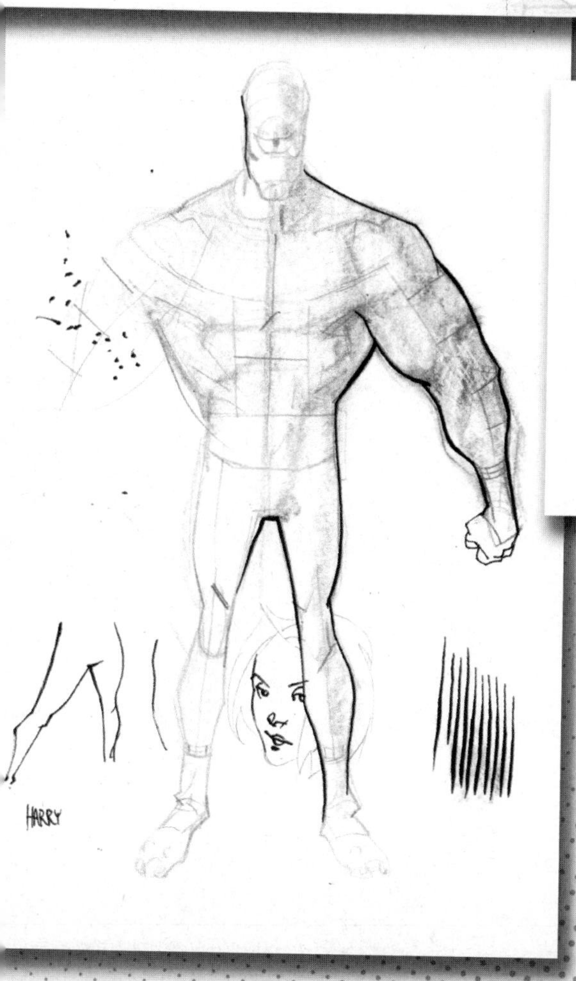
HARRY

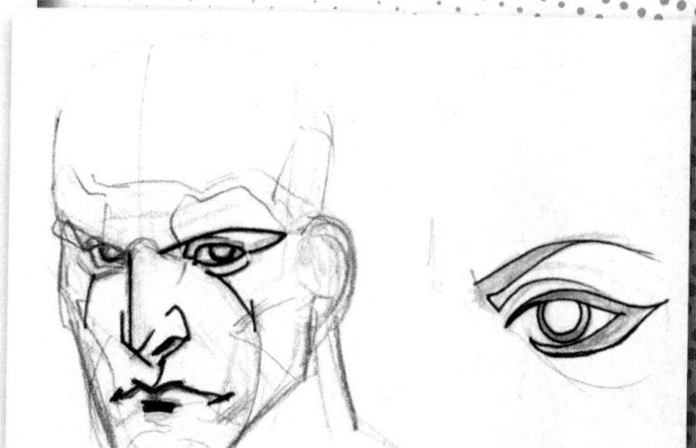

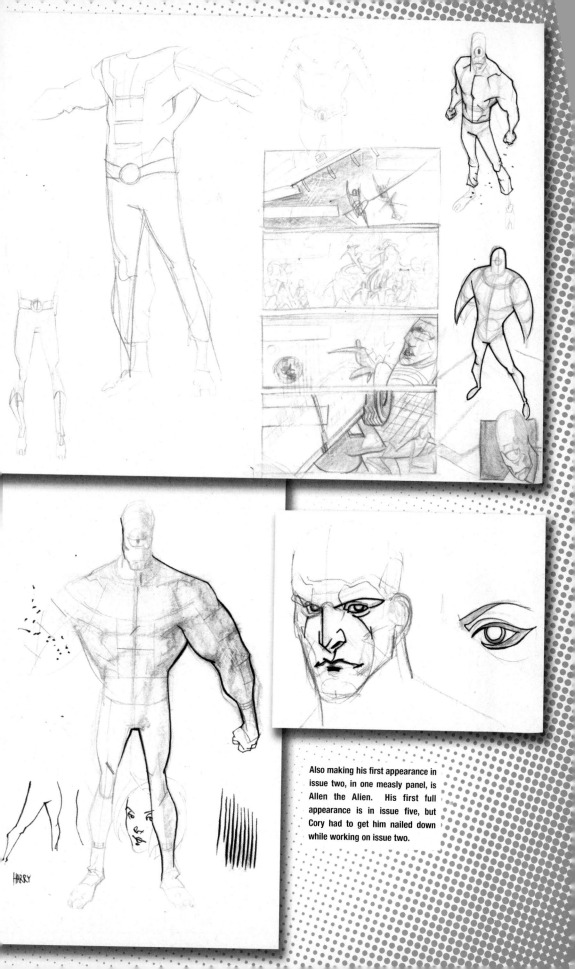

Also making his first appearance in issue two, in one measly panel, is Allen the Alien. His first full appearance is in issue five, but Cory had to get him nailed down while working on issue two.

On this page we see some designs for Mauler, as well as the supporting character William. When we started working on issue one I told Bill Crabtree that I'd try to get Cory to throw him in the book. I think that's always fun to do, and people seem to enjoy it. When I decided which character to make Bill, it was just one of Mark's friends from high school... no big deal. At the time I had forgotten that I had big plans for the guy... so now Bill Crabtree himself is a major supporting character in one of the books he colors.

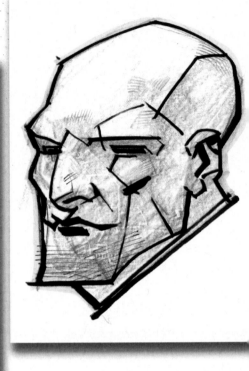

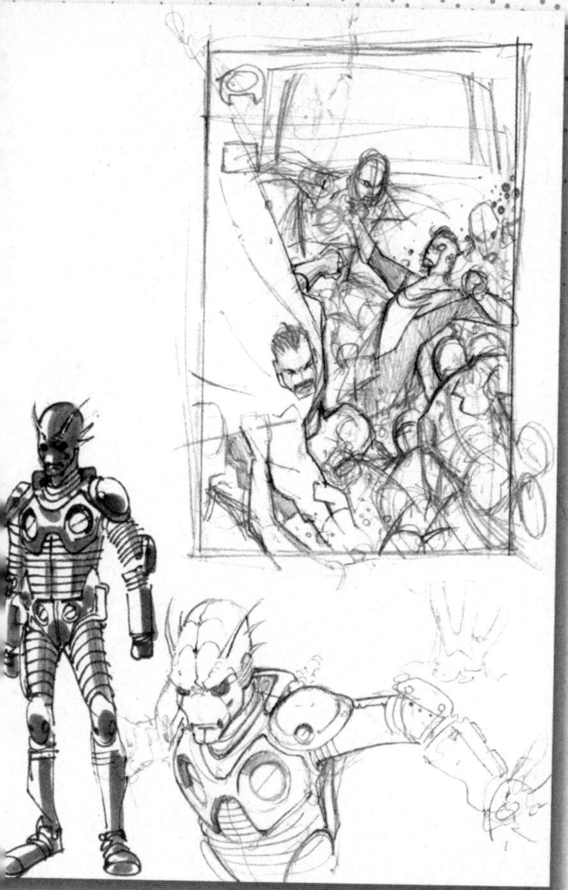

Here we see some designs for the aliens in issue 3... still no name for those guys. Also seen here, the cover sketch for the cover of this very trade. It's based on a suggestion Kurt Busiek had for the cover of issue 2. He didn't seem too keen on most of the covers we did in this arc so I asked him to tell me what he would have done to try and get a feel for what he thought was a good cover. When he suggested this one I thought it would be perfect for the trade. Cory and Bill really hit this one out of the park... I just love how the cover for this book turned out.

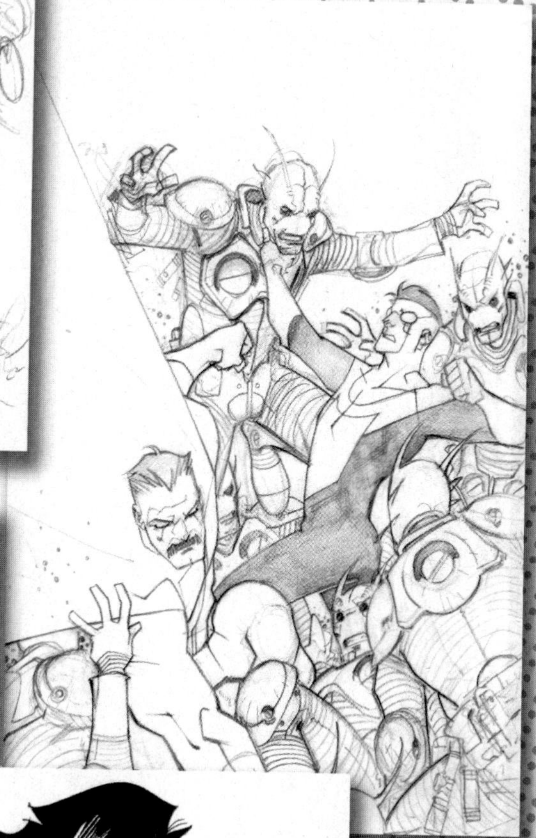

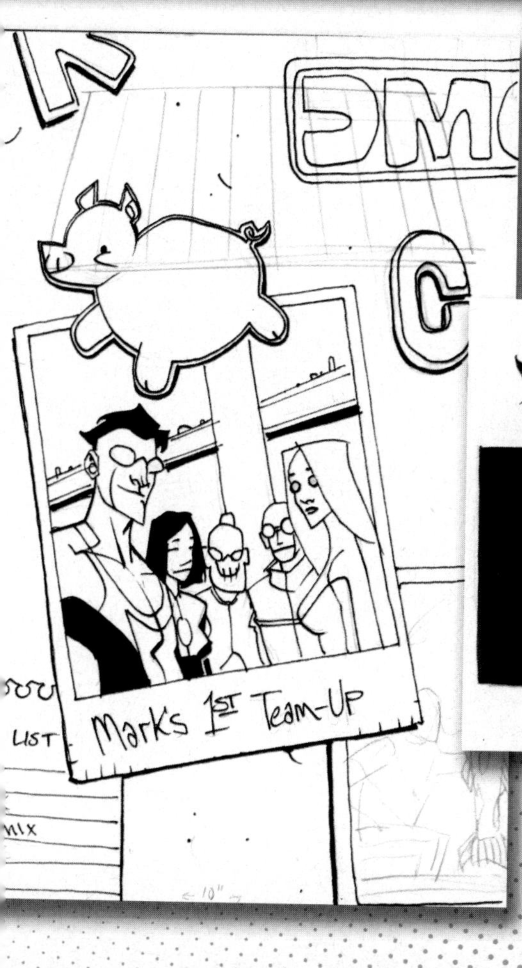
Mark's 1st Team-Up

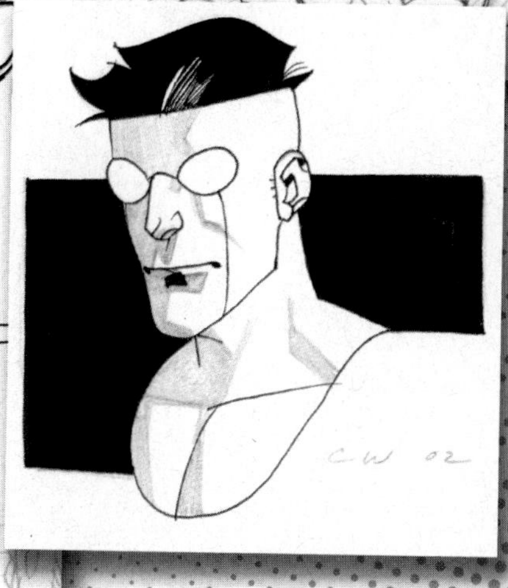
C.W. 02

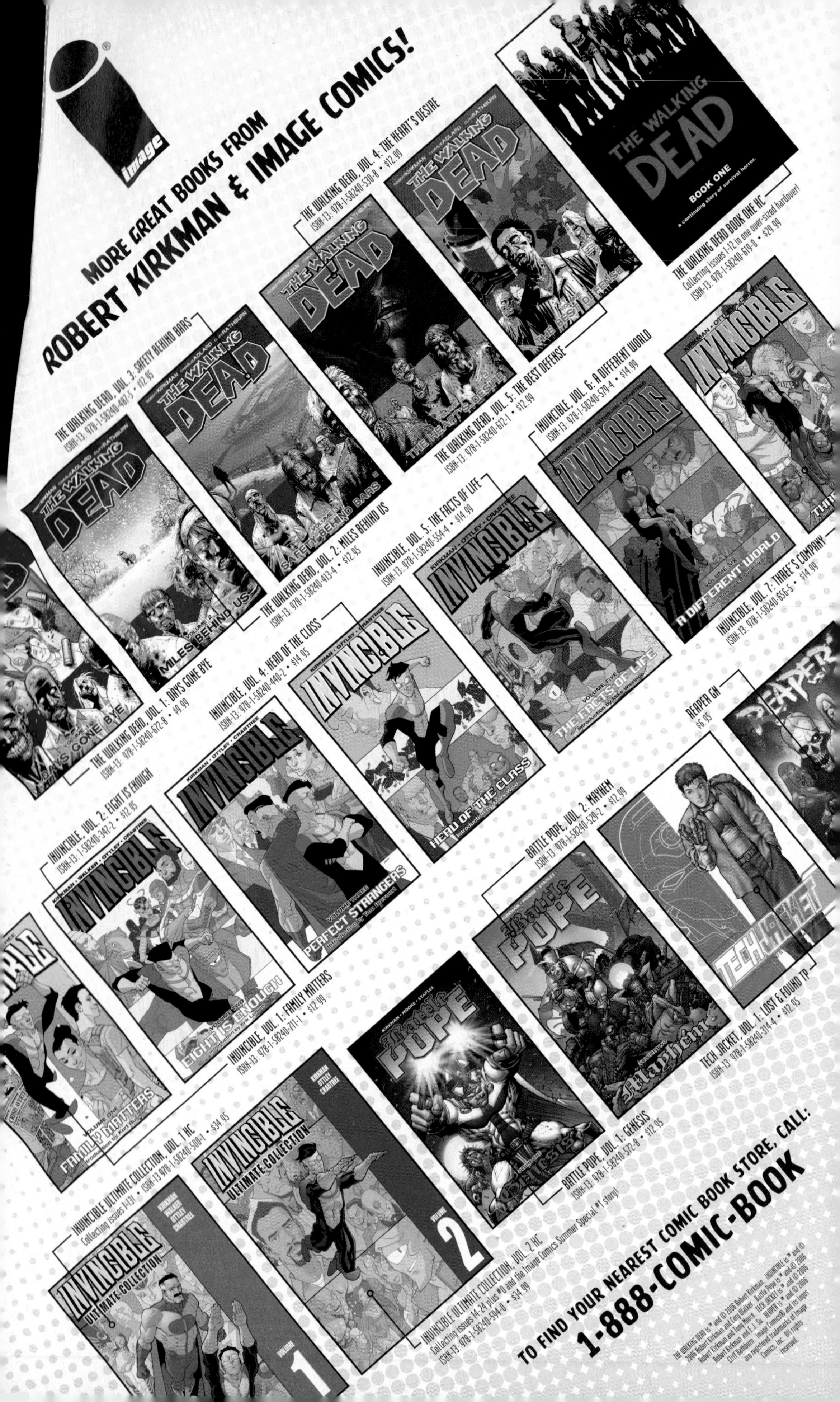

MORE GREAT BOOKS FROM
ROBERT KIRKMAN & IMAGE COMICS!
THE WALKING DEAD BOOK ONE HC
Collecting issues 1-12 in one over-sized hardover!
ISBN-13: 978-1-58240-619-0 • $29.99
THE WALKING DEAD, VOL. 1: DAYS GONE BYE
ISBN-13: 978-1-58240-672-8 • $9.99
THE WALKING DEAD, VOL. 2: MILES BEHIND US
ISBN-13: 978-1-58240-413-4 • $12.95
THE WALKING DEAD, VOL. 3: SAFETY BEHIND BARS
ISBN-13: 978-1-58240-487-5 • $12.95
THE WALKING DEAD, VOL. 4: THE HEART'S DESIRE
ISBN-13: 978-1-58240-530-8 • $12.99
THE WALKING DEAD, VOL. 5: THE BEST DEFENSE
ISBN-13: 978-1-58240-612-1 • $12.99
INVINCIBLE, VOL. 1: FAMILY MATTERS
ISBN-13: 978-1-58240-711-1 • $12.99
INVINCIBLE, VOL. 2: EIGHT IS ENOUGH
ISBN-13: 1-58240-347-2 • $12.95
INVINCIBLE, VOL. 4: HEAD OF THE CLASS
ISBN-13: 978-1-58240-440-2 • $14.95
INVINCIBLE, VOL. 5: THE FACTS OF LIFE
ISBN-13: 978-1-58240-554-4 • $14.99
INVINCIBLE, VOL. 6: A DIFFERENT WORLD
ISBN-13: 978-1-58240-579-4 • $14.99
INVINCIBLE, VOL. 7: THREE'S COMPANY
ISBN-13: 978-1-58240-656-5 • $14.99
REAPER GN
$6.95
BATTLE POPE, VOL. 1: GENESIS
ISBN-13: 978-1-58240-572-8 • $12.95
BATTLE POPE, VOL. 2: MAYHEM
ISBN-13: 978-1-58240-529-2 • $12.99
TECH JACKET, VOL. 1: LOST & FOUND TP
ISBN-13: 978-1-58240-314-4 • $12.95
INVINCIBLE ULTIMATE COLLECTION, VOL. 1 HC
Collecting issues 1-13! • ISBN-13 978-1-58240-500-1 • $34.95
INVINCIBLE ULTIMATE COLLECTION, VOL. 2 HC
Collecting issues 14-24 plus #0 and the Image Comics Summer Special #1 story!
ISBN-13: 978-1-58240-594-0 • $34.99
TO FIND YOUR NEAREST COMIC BOOK STORE, CALL:
1-888-COMIC-BOOK
THE WALKING DEAD is ™ and © 2006 Robert Kirkman. INVINCIBLE is ™ and © 2006 Robert Kirkman and Cory Walker. Battle Pope is ™ and © 2006 Robert Kirkman and Tony Moore. TECH JACKET is ™ and © 2006 Robert Kirkman and E.J. Su. REAPER is ™ and © 2006 Cliff Rathburn. Image Comics® and its logos are registered trademarks of Image Comics, Inc. All rights reserved.